A NOVEL

witness

in

the

DARK

Lynne Larson

Covenant Communications, Inc.

Published by Covenant Communications, Inc.
American Fork, Utah

Printed in the United States of America
First Printing: January 2017

22 21 20 19 18 17   10 9 8 7 6 5 4 3 2 1

ISBN-13: 978-1-52440-184-9

witness

in

the

DARK

OTHER BOOKS AND AUDIO BOOKS
BY LYNNE LARSON:

In the Shadow of an Angel

Saving Lucie Cole

Another Time for Love

Loving Leah

For Brett and Beau,
a mother's cherished boys

Chapter One

JENNIFER BRODIE TOPPLED HEAD FIRST and backwards into the gaping hole with nothing below her but a narrow, blind shaft, black as pitch and deep as a bedrock well. She hadn't been prepared for disaster. Two minutes earlier she'd no idea it was going to happen.

Jennifer was not yet twenty, still a kid to people in Tooele. Out of school and home for the summer, the pretty, straight-haired blonde had modeled for the local Buckskin and Barrel catalog, showing off blue jeans and belt buckles for this season's county fair. She was a familiar face folks smiled at, proud of their hometown sweetheart, brainy enough for BYU and a nice-looking girl, besides. You couldn't do much better, people said, but Jenny didn't hear them. She was guileless, which made this sudden, life-threatening crisis seem all the more unfair.

On horseback again after several months away from the family spread, a glorious season stretched in front of her. She was the bishop's daughter, the girl next door. Slim and sunny and brown-eyed, she wore a red-checked cotton shirt and a stiff-brimmed hat, without a care in the world or a desperate cause to fight for. How was she to know she was going to open the wrong door that morning and face a scene out of some horror picture? How was *anyone* to know that the rolling hills and cloudless sky of Tooele County would hold a secret by nightfall, and a community would be weeping as it searched frantically for one of its own?

When she saw the scene, all Jennifer could do was turn and run. She did have the presence of mind to grab little Clara's hand and block her from the view, but after grizzled Luther Grunwald began to yell and come after them with fire in his eyes, Jennifer forgot everything but raw survival. Clara struggled free and headed in the other direction, a confused and clueless child, but Jennifer kept running until Luther caught up with her about twenty-five yards from the barn. He was devil-bent on stopping a chance eyewitness to a murder—*his* murder of Bill Muncie, a man who was once a well-respected business partner to the mayor—and it pushed him all the harder. Screaming while Luther tried to clap a greasy hand across her mouth, Jennifer fought him like a wildcat, clawing and scratching and jerking and kicking with every ounce of strength she had, which wasn't nearly enough. Jenny Brodie was just a girl, all of 110 pounds. Grunwald's hands were large, his muscles hard and strong. Jenny Brodie never had a chance.

***

Of course, from Luther Grunwald's point of view, he wasn't to blame at all . . .

Luther dropped the gun a split second after he'd shot Bill Muncie. After that, his only weapon was his muscle—his fists and the hundred pounds he had on Jennifer, who had no business being where she didn't belong. That's the way he saw it. In the end, he didn't have to use his fists. He never had to hit the girl at all. He simply had to catch her. He managed that because he knew the place better than she ever could. Chasing her through the wide back gate where things looked deceivingly clear, he knew he had her cornered. She had nowhere to go. The shaft was handy, and in panic and frustration, he dragged her toward its mouth. He had to quiet her and quickly, with the least amount of trouble. She was light to lift, but she was still wiggling and noisy, scratching and biting. So he stood over the opening of the shaft and didn't take too long to think about it. Somewhat like a fellow might throw a sack of potatoes down the cellar stairs, he pushed her over the edge and dropped her down before she could grip his shirt or hang on to his collar or gulp enough air to make her last squeal of terror heard.

There was more surprise in her eyes than anything, Luther would remember, at least at first. Only one shrill gasp of panic as she fell backwards into the darkness. One gasp and nothing more. He had stood there a moment to catch his breath and listen and look for any signs of the struggle. Things were calm and clean. There was barely a rise in the dust around the hole. No clattering, no call for help, no ringing echo from the bottom of the shaft. No disturbance of whatever moldered there. Only silence. The scene appeared the same as it had always been, stark but quietly benign.

Finally, Luther Grunwald had straightened his shoulders and wiped his brow with his sleeve. He was a late-forties man of average to thick build, a leathery fellow who had tufts of pale hair sticking out from underneath his crumpled hat. He tinkered with old cars and earned money fixing small engines when he could. He and Clara lived in an old trailer on the Muncie lot, which included a sagging barn and some other outbuildings. The pit was an old mine shaft on the edge of the property. A flimsy rope was pulled across the opposite side. The shaft was one of many that dotted the vast prairie west of the populated Wasatch Front in Utah. Ranchers and herders here were used to the "holes" from a bygone era. Most, long abandoned, were not that deep or dangerous. Some ran horizontally into the sides of bluffs and mesas. A few were vertical and dropped deep into the earth. Spelunkers visited them for fun; geologists and historians visited them out of curiosity and for research. But this one near the Muncie place had been forgotten long ago.

The guilty man surveyed his surroundings. The shaft was below a pile of boulders that rose up just outside the Muncie property line. Yards away, closer to the barn, a row of scraggly poplar trees stood sentinel in the sun. Between the two points, a ditch ran along a fringe of grass where a few chickens usually clustered. The skeletons of three wrecked cars rusted in the weeds that lined the approaching road, a dirt trail off the paved highway. Farther, toward the sun, beyond the fertile hills and trees, Utah's great West Desert stretched, a vast wasteland of sage and sand, the devil's pasture. Grunwald knew no one had observed him from that direction.

Grunwald wondered vacantly where Clara was and if she had seen what had just occurred. He knew she was likely peeking out from behind some corner, staring mutely with those bug-like eyes of hers, so strange. Luther Grunwald hadn't begun his morning expecting to be a murderer. He hadn't planned to shoot Bill Muncie, and he didn't generally raise a hand against a woman. But Jennifer Brodie was an accidental witness to what he'd done, and she ran away before he had any time to think. Besides that, she kicked and scratched and clawed at him. She bit his finger when he tried to smother her screams. He had to put a stop to all of that. His actions were in self-defense, he told himself, and he had the marks and welts to prove it. He'd only done what was necessary, and no one was going to tell him otherwise.

Nosy neighbors anyway! What was the girl even doing in his barn? That was the question. He hadn't asked for any of this!

After peering intently one more time into the dark eye of the shaft, Luther Grunwald turned and walked away, bent on finding Clara and Jennifer Brodie's saddle pony, which, along with the body of Bill Muncie, needed to be moved off his place and soon.

Chapter Two

IT WAS THE TUMBLEWEEDS THAT saved Jennifer Brodie. The giant, airy, buoyant tumbleweeds that bounce along the wind like loose balloons escaped from a prairie circus. Luther Grunwald himself had stuffed a few of them in the pit one forgotten blustery day when he was clearing the yard after a dust-up. The lip of the shaft had captured more on its own, sucking them in when they bounced too close and lingered too long over the hole. The tangle of round bushes sank far enough down the tight shaft to provide a stack of branches at the bottom, fifty feet from its mouth. The deceptively stickery weeds were no soft cushion, but they were a cushion nonetheless. Jennifer landed hard against them, ending up unconscious, badly bruised and bleeding, but alive.

No one knows quite how to deal with a life-and-death crisis, especially at nineteen years old when it comes whirling out of the blue on a bright summer day. A typical moment turns to terror in one split second. The world's a beautiful place, and then it isn't. As the hours passed, Jennifer lay cradled in the darkness among the tumbleweeds while a thousand images flooded though her brain. Daddy! Momma! Dillon, Tony . . . Clara? There were patterns of light, flashes of comprehension, glimpses of memory, and then nothing but fog and shadow—and pain, agonizing pain, knifing through her ears and over the crown of her head. At times she tried to scream but somehow had no strength to do it. She tried to open her eyes, to find out where she was, but she couldn't seem to do that either. Except for the occasional dream-like sparks of light, which flooded her mind and not her eyes, she was bound and trapped by gloom, figuratively and otherwise. Still, she struggled to make sense of it. *Where was she? What had happened, and how did it all begin?*

Back two days from BYU . . . Yes, she could remember now. She was at the dinner table, and the house was warm with familiar colors and the smell of her mother's cooking. Her father, Rex Brodie, sprang a question on her. She could hear his voice, so full and deep and pleasant. Yes, she could remember . . .

"How would you like to help out in the Primary while you're home this summer, Jen? Sister Allen says she needs a CTR teacher." It was more than an inquiry, since Jennifer's father was *Bishop* Brodie of the Sunset Second Ward, Rolling Desert Stake, on the outskirts of Tooele, but Jen was eager with an answer.

"Oh, I'd love to do it." She looked up from her enchiladas, her favorite and a homecoming treat for dinner. "That would be so fun. How old are CTRs, now? I've forgotten."

"Well, it depends," said her mother, cheerily passing more sour cream. "You know, there's CTR 4, CTR 5, CTR 6 and so on. They make up about half the Primary." Evelyn Brodie, a trim brunette, beamed at Jen from across the table. Provo wasn't that far away, but she was thrilled to have her daughter completely home for the summer and not just an occasional weekend visit. Ah, the months ahead would be glorious!

"What about Dillon?" Jennifer's dirty-blond, spikey-haired brother, sixteen-year-old Tony, shot a smirk in her direction.

"Dillon?" The bishop shrugged, a twinkle in his eye. "What *about* Dillon? I think Sister Allen would rather have Jen teach the CTRs."

"Yeah, but how is Dillon going to hold Jennifer's hand in Sunday School if she's stuck in the Primary?" teased Tony. "Life just isn't fair, is it, sis?"

"Dillon sees enough of Jenny every night," said Bishop Brodie. "He can let the Primary have her on Sunday."

"I'll be clerking at Dudley's as well," Jennifer said, "so I'll be plenty busy weekdays too."

"Dillon may be more occupied himself this summer," the bishop added as he ate. "I hear he's hired on as a deputy with Sheriff Castle, since Mitch Kilroy broke his leg. Len Gardner is still the main guy, but Dill will tag along."

"Jen, is that right?" Evelyn was surprised. "I didn't know Dill was interested in law enforcement."

"It's just a summer job, Momma," Jen told her quickly. "His uncle got it for him. Dill says it'll help him save for his mission."

"Yes." Bishop Brodie winked, reaching over to tweak his daughter's ear. "And hopefully keep him off our front porch at two a.m. sweet-talkin' my baby girl."

"They're doin' more than talkin'," laughed Tony. Then he grabbed his leg and winced in mock agony as Jen nudged him hard underneath the table.

"Come on, you two," said Evelyn to her husband and her son. "Give Dill and Jen a break. She's been gone so long in

Provo, and him stuck here working with his dad. Let them get a little 'cozy' while they can. "

"Momma!" Jen was horrified . . . and a little delighted.

"What? What did I say?" laughed Evelyn, who, like most mothers, knew Jennifer better than Jen knew herself. "You don't think *I've* been down that road?" She shot a mischievous glance at her husband.

"Well, any 'coziness' with Dill Dancie had better be *very* short term," declared the bishop. "His mission call awaits!"

"Don't worry, Dad," said Jennifer. "A little summer romance won't be a problem. Those things never last."

Jen wasn't sure how she felt long term about Dillon Dancie. He was certainly still the gorgeous guy back home she'd told her Provo friends about, blond and square-jawed and firmly built. Close friends since junior high school and dating all through high school, they weren't officially engaged, but everyone in town considered them a couple. There was no doubt she liked him well enough, but the past year at BYU had changed her outlook a little. She worried sometimes about getting between Dill and his mission, and then she worried about him forgetting her while he was gone. Most of all, she wondered if he truly loved her or was it simply kisses and caresses on the front porch swing? Maybe that was all he really loved. How was a girl to ever know for sure?

Dillon, are you there? Can you get me out of here? Get my dad to help you. It's so dark and cold, and I can't see anything. Daddy . . . I'll hang on till you come.

Jennifer talked to Marie Allen the next day, stopping at the Primary president's house, and Sister Allen greeted her like she was truly the answer to a week of prayer and fasting. "Oh, my gosh, am I glad to see *you*!" Sister Allen cried, embracing Jen and explaining the Primary's need at a harried ninety miles plus per hour. It was CTR 6 where Jennifer could be put to best use, Sister Allen said. There were at least eight precious children there without a teacher for the summer. Amy Tillotson's twins had come early, and no one knew how long she was going to be in Salt Lake at the neo-natal care unit or how long she'd be homebound with the babies after that. So Jennifer was a godsend. The lesson for the coming Sunday was on the Old Testament story of Joseph and his coat of many colors. Sister Allen had already looked it up. Jennifer could go online, or she could take the lesson book and all the printed supplementary material Sister Allen was handing her. Her class would be in charge of Sharing Time the last Sunday in June, and Activity Days were every other Tuesday. The Primary was preparing a special children's concert with the stake for the Pioneer Day celebration this year, and rehearsals were every Thursday afternoon at three, beginning the middle of June. If there was anything she needed or any questions, she shouldn't hesitate to ask.

Between several grateful hugs from Sister Allen and reassurances that the children would love her as a substitute for Sister Tillotson, Jennifer took the material, promised to go online, and managed to escape the Allen living room before the woman's excited chatter made her late for work.

Later, at home, Jen dug through her mother's yardage cupboard and found enough colorful strips to sew a little cape together, one complete with sparkles and stars, and good enough to stand in as a coat of many colors for a six-year-old. She was rather proud of her efforts until she paraded the creation past the family and Tony offered his usual snide critique. "You know, they say that visual aids are sometimes simply a cover for poor teaching."

"Gee, thanks." Jennifer rolled her eyes.

"Just sayin'," Tony teased. "If Joseph was wearin' anything like that cape of yours, it's no wonder his brothers threw him in a pit."

She gave him a playful punch in the shoulder but later conceded to her father that she had her doubts about the lesson. "These kids are six years old," she worried. "It's hard to talk about Joseph's brothers wanting to kill him over a coat. The lesson softens that part of the story, and I will, too, of course, but I still want to get the point across of how Joseph was mistreated because of petty jealousy by those who should have loved him."

They were in Bishop Brodie's office at home, Jen remembered, a study where all his books surrounded them with golden letters on the spines. The books had intrigued her since she'd been a little girl and had probably first given her the urge to read and learn and understand the world. A year at BYU had only added fuel to that fire. But it dawned on her that maybe she was overdoing things with the cape.

"Don't let Tony's teasing get to you," said her father gently. "I think your coat of many colors looks fantastic, and so does Tony, if he'd admit it."

"I guess so, Dad," replied Jen, seeing her father with new admiration. He was a distinguished-looking man, this dad of hers, with strong features, bright eyes, and a thick head of hair just beginning to gray. Being away had taught her to appreciate him.

Rex Brodie was sitting at his desk, Jennifer across from him. He paused and contemplated her a moment with a certain paternal tenderness he didn't often show. "What are you planning to go into down there at BYU? Have you decided?"

Jen was a bit surprised. "I don't know yet. Freshman year you just worry about the basics. I love it there; I'll tell you that." She paused, musing. "I thought I was so smart getting into BYU, and here I am struggling to come up with a decent Primary lesson, one that will really help the kids." She suddenly caught herself and laughed at her own penchant for taking things too seriously. "I've got a lot to learn," she said aloud and gestured in the direction of the countless volumes spread about the room. "I don't know if I'll live long enough to make it."

Live long enough? Will I live long enough to make it out of here? It's so dark. Where am I anyway?

Rex Brodie chuckled. "Let's just worry about the Primary lesson for now. Wait here a minute. I think I've got something you can use."

Her father got up and left the room while Jennifer pushed everything on the desk to one side. Her Primary materials were there but nothing else. It was late. Dill was working a dusk-to-dawn patrol for Sheriff Castle. Rex brought a leather pouch back into the room and dumped a pile of silver dollars in front of his daughter. "I've been saving these for a while," he said. "Some of them are kind of old, but there's nothing really special about them. It's just that you don't see a silver dollar all that often, especially ones like these. A couple of 'em are what we call Lady Dollars or Peace Dollars, the ones with Liberty on them. They were minted in 1921. Not many of them are still around, but you see 'em every now and then.

"How many have you got here, Dad?" Jen began counting. There were a few Susan B. Anthony dollars, but most were modern pieces. There were three Peace Dollars with the face of Lady Liberty on them. Forty-seven silver pieces altogether.

"I've picked them up here and there. Sometimes when we've traveled through Nevada and other places. You can get them at banks sometimes if you ask. They're heavy, so most people don't care to have too many around. I just keep 'em for a hobby mostly. The older ones are the most valuable."

Jen juggled several of the dollars in her palm. "How long have you had these?"

"Ten, twelve years maybe. I don't know."

"Cool."

"Now, here's what I think you could do for your class," her father told her. "The lesson says Joseph's brothers sold him to the merchants for twenty pieces of silver. You take twenty of these dollars, put them in this pouch, and tell the kids this is like the silver the brothers got—twenty pieces of silver for a boy they should have loved and protected. Instead, they put him in a pit until they could sell him for a little bit of silver." Jennifer's father took her hand and dropped a stack of dollars into her palm—twenty of them. "Even those six-year-olds will see it's not a lot of money."

"I probably shouldn't take your older dollars, Dad," said Jen, seeing one of the coins she had was a Peace Dollar. "They're too valuable."

"Don't worry about that," said the bishop. "It's for a good cause; they're all the same to me." He folded her fingers over the coins she held. She got the message. This visual aid was better than the coat.

They put him in a pit, in a pit, in a pit, in a pit, in a pit. . . . Jen wondered if the pit was dark like hers and if it too smelled like dead animals.

Sunday went very well. Dillon was at church and looked tall and filled out his striking blue suit nicely. His cheeks were high and tan, his short curly hair slightly disheveled. He held her hand during sacrament meeting, and people smiled at them and went out of their way to welcome her back. It was fun to be in her home ward again with all its familiar, friendly faces. Sunset Second wasn't Dill's ward, but he had dated Jennifer so long everybody knew him. She had hoped he would go with her to BYU or leave on his mission as soon as he turned eighteen. But his family had run into financial problems when a business partner died, and Dillon was needed at home. Prospects had improved since then, and the mission would come in the fall. Dill was a year behind in life, and he had already told her nervously, "You're growing up while I'm sitting on my hands. I'm scared to death of losing you."

Losing you, losing you, losing you, losing you. . . . She whispered them, but the words echoed off the sides of the pit and were lost in the darkness. Jennifer, her head throbbing, her senses whirling, worked frantically to call them back. As reality returned, however, pain and fear sharpened as well, so slips in and out of consciousness remained a welcome pause.

Clara Grunwald came to Primary. It had never happened before, at least not that anyone could remember, and Marie Allen was certain it wouldn't happen again very soon. But that Sunday, the day Jennifer told the story about Joseph and his brothers, Clara Grunwald came. She was the oddest little girl Jennifer had ever seen. She had pale, coarse hair, which hung like frayed rope on either side of her sallow cheeks, and her mouth remained in a perpetual flatline of inexpression on her angular face. Her wide-set eyes were large and blue, and they gazed so intently at whatever they looked upon, their glare was almost startling. She wore a shabby sundress with a print of faded flowers. It rode up above her brown legs when she sat on the folding classroom chairs and revealed skinned knees. The soiled little slippers on her feet displayed ragged holes worn through the toes. In her fist she clutched a soiled rag doll with a missing button eye and scrawny threads of yarn simulating hair. Jennifer felt a well of sympathy for the child.

"Hello, Clara. I'm so glad you came today," she said brightly. Marie Allen had told Jen who the girl was, and Jen made a point to welcome her to class and bend down to speak to her at her own level in the circle where the children sat.

The girl frowned at the greeting, as if Jennifer had slapped her.

"She's deaf and dumb," the boy next to Clara announced loudly, and Clara promptly turned and scowled at him, raising a small clenched fist. Her bulging eyes looked as though they would momentarily catch fire.

"No. No, she's not," said Jennifer quickly. "She's a *very* pretty girl." Tweaking the child's chin in a friendly way, she hoped her tone would communicate the kindness she sincerely felt. She knew Clara Grunwald was mute—"She doesn't speak at all," Sister Allen had told her—but she *could* hear, and she certainly wasn't dumb! "You can almost see the wheels spinning behind those piercing eyes of hers." The Primary president was careful to add, "She understands every word you say."

"I'm shocked to see her here," the first counselor had whispered during opening exercises. "Her mother's dead, and her father never comes. I don't think he's even a member. Likely he just dropped poor little Clara off because he wanted to go to town and hit the pool hall with his friends or something. It's a shame, but that's my guess."

Whatever the reason she was there that day, little Clara Grunwald kept her brows sternly pinched, and her lips twisted a quizzical frown all through the lesson about Joseph being put into a pit before being sold by his brothers. "At least some of the brothers probably felt sorry for Joseph while he was in the pit," Jennifer suggested in her kindest tone. "What do you think those brothers could have done to help him?"

At first most of the six-year-olds seemed stupefied by the question and gazed back at Jennifer as if she'd just called on them to solve the riddle of the ages. Then one little boy said, "Water. They should bring him water." Another added, "Food," and soon several children in the circle joined the chorus, suggesting, among other things, a "cover" so Joseph could keep warm and a pillow for his head. Then suddenly everyone fell silent and turned together to one end of the semicircle, where little Clara Grunwald was holding out her doll.

"That's silly," giggled the Bradshaw boy, a red-haired little fellow with a cowlick and a perfectly knotted tie. "Joseph wouldn't want a doll!" The children laughed, fidgeting on their chairs and dubiously eyeing Clara's proffered doll like it was some kind of rat.

Jennifer was quick to rescue her. "Oh, I think that's a great idea, Clara. Our toys can often be a comfort to us when we're lost or lonely. I know if I were in a pit, I'd want my favorite doll with me!"

She was worried that the little girl wouldn't respond again, since she'd been laughed at, but Clara's bulging eyes gleamed when she saw the money Jennifer poured from Bishop Brodie's pouch. She seemed to count each dollar. Jen told the children what the money represented in the story, and she sensed that the little girl had never in her life seen even one silver dollar, let alone so much money altogether.

When Primary was over and the other children had scrambled from the room, Clara Grunwald remained, staring at Jennifer with that inscrutable expression, not friendly, not loving or kind or grateful, just strange and empty of anything childlike or fragile.

"I'm glad you came today, Clara," Jennifer repeated when they were alone and the girl just sat in her chair still staring at the pouch of silver dollars on the table. "Do you think you'll come next time?"

Clara lowered her eyes and shrugged. Her frayed hair stood out like straw, covering her ears. Jennifer wished she had an extra brush and a pretty ribbon in her tote bag to perhaps tie back the strands.

"I'd certainly like to see you again next week. I'll be teaching the class all summer, so we can become good friends."

Clara's eyes returned to the pouch, and Jennifer's heart, which had been at the breaking point all day, finally melted. She opened the bag and took out a silver dollar, the Peace Dollar. Clara seemed to like that one, perhaps because of the woman's face on it. "She's pretty, isn't she?" said Jen. "She's Lady Liberty. Great name, huh?" Taking the girl's small hand in her own, she placed the coin in the little palm. "Here," she said, "you keep this. It's just for you. Don't tell anyone else about it. Buy something special with it someday, or don't. It's up to you. Every girl should have something shiny that belongs only to her. And if a great lady's picture's on it, that makes it all the better!"

Even this gesture brought no smile from strange little Clara, but she turned the dollar over in her hands as if it were warm to the touch. Then, suddenly, as if she was afraid this crazy Primary teacher might change her mind, she dashed past Jennifer, out of the room, and down the hallway to the nearest outside door, never looking back, clutching her rag doll and her silver dollar.

A few minutes later in the parking lot, Jennifer caught a glimpse of Clara Grunwald climbing into a big grimy truck driven by a sour-looking man in a rumpled hat, presumably her father. The truck's blue paint was crusted with rust, and at least two windows were cracked and taped into their frames.

Scraped and dented from fan to fender, the truck labored under a burdensome load. Some kind of heavy machinery weighed down the bed, and when Clara settled into her seat, Jen could see there was barely room for her. Miscellaneous blankets and boxes filled the cab.

She watched all of this over Dillon's shoulder as she stood telling him good-bye beside his car. He was leaving to pull a Sunday shift for Sheriff Castle. "The ox is always in the mire when you're the low man at the station," Dillon joked, his eyes never leaving hers. "I'll run home, change clothes, and be on patrol till midnight." He was devilishly handsome in his crisp blue suit and silk necktie. Jen had always loved his tight-clipped, curly hair, and she could hardly take her eyes away from him now. His folks were out of town, and Jen had hoped they could spend the afternoon together. Now she was disappointed. Momentarily forgetting Clara Grunwald, she slid her fingers up and down Dill's blue lapel. "I guess you'll miss my mother's Sunday chicken," she purred. "Stop over at the house on your dinner break, and I'll warm you up a plate."

"That's an offer I can't refuse." Dill grinned, touching noses gently with her before he backed away.

Did you come for dinner, Dill? I can't remember. It's so dark in here; I don't know where I am. My mind is swimming. I've got to figure out what happened and why there's so much pain. Help me, Dad or Dill or anybody . . . someone, please.

Chapter Three

"YOU GAVE THAT WEIRD LITTLE Grunwald girl one of Dad's silver dollars?!" Tony was full of mock indignation at the Brodie dinner table.

"Now, Tony," scolded Evelyn, "I'm sure Jen knew a teaching moment when she saw one."

"I'm sorry, Dad," said Jen with genuine remorse. "And it was the Peace Dollar, too, because she liked that one. I probably shouldn't have done it since I gave nothing to the other kids, but I felt so darn sorry for this little girl. You should have seen her. I'll bet she's never held a *nickel* in her fingers, let alone a dollar. It was worth it just to see her eyes light up. I'll pay you back. I promise."

"No need," said Bishop Brodie, listening pleasantly.

"So your lesson went well, I take it?" Evelyn smiled.

"Oh, I guess," Jennifer replied, not completely convinced. "I told the story, and when I asked at the end why the pouch of silver pieces was important, all the kids just sat there, blank as posts. I said, 'Do you see how these few silver pieces weren't worth anything compared to the life of Joseph, the brother that these men sold?' And all the kids just sat there and stared at me as if they didn't know what I was talking about." Jennifer stirred her salad a moment with her fork and then added, a bit forlornly, "Then that Bradshaw boy, the one with the red hair—"

"The one who thinks he knows more than the teacher because his family has family home evening *every* week," said Tony, "and he's only six?"

"Wait till he's twelve." The bishop winked. "He *will* know more than most of them."

"Yeah, that's the one," continued Jen. "I asked, 'Do you see how the silver pieces weren't worth anything compared to the life of Joseph?' and the Bradshaw boy says, 'The coins *were* worth a lot. The bad brothers wanted the money. Those silver pieces were what got Joseph out of the pit!'"

"I'll be darn," said Bishop Brodie after a pause. "That's pretty good for a six-year-old."

"It didn't do my lesson any favors," said Jennifer, thinking of the way Clara had scowled at the boy as if he had just arrived from another planet.

"We never know about talks and lessons and the words that stick with people," remarked the bishop, shrugging it off. "We never know."

Early that evening, she was taking Dill's warmed-up chicken out of the oven and Dill was at the dining room table making friendly with her father when Clara Grunwald's name came up again. Actually, it was the Grunwalds' landlord, Bill Muncie, Dill first mentioned, asking Rex if he'd seen the rancher lately.

"Can't say as I have," answered the bishop. "But Muncie comes and goes. Since his divorce, he doesn't really live here anymore, you know. Although, he's around enough, checking on his holdings. Why you want to know?"

Dill smiled up at Jen as she set his plate in front of him. "Sheriff Castle got word that UHP picked Muncie up on I-80 the other day, just this side of Wendover, driving a Plymouth with stolen tags. Muncie pleaded ignorance, said he'd borrowed the car, and got off with a warning. But the state cops asked Castle to look into those junk heaps at Grunwald's, which is where Bill claimed to have got the Plymouth."

"Yeah, Mike Castle called me about making a welfare check at Grunwald's," said Bishop Brodie. He glanced at Jennifer, who'd sat down next to Dill. "We've both been worried about that little girl."

"Clara?" wondered Jen, with widening eyes.

"She missed a lot of days last month before school got out. There's no mother there, just her and the father, which is no crime, certainly, but possibly hard on the child." The bishop looked suddenly up at Jennifer. "I've been thinking about it, Jen, and I'd like to take you with me. The little girl knows you now as her Primary teacher. It'll make things easier."

"Sure, of course," said Jen, surprised and pleased that her father would ask.

"Sheriff Castle has a couple of concerns there at the Grunwald place," put in Dill between his bites of chicken dumpling. "Besides the rusted jalopies Grunwald's got sitting around, which may or may not be stolen, I guess there's an old mine shaft nearby that Muncie should have plugged up a long time ago just for safety's sake. Castle probably thinks he can use the welfare visit as a cover for the other stuff. You know, kill lots of birds with just one stone."

"Well, let's hope killing's not a part of anything," Bishop Brodie smiled, "not with a child anywhere around."

Killing? Yes, something awful happened. She was beginning to remember now. There was a gunshot. Little Clara running.

Was it Luther Grunwald's hand across her mouth? She kicked and scratched and twisted and bit down hard. But then the collapse came, the reaching out into the darkness when nothing was there to grasp.

They followed a dirt road three miles west of town the following Tuesday, midmorning. Jen was working the late shift at Dudley's Desert Boutique that day, and Castle said morning was a good time for him, so that's when they met— Jen and her father in one car, Dill and Castle in another. Dill and the sheriff were in uniform but unarmed. "We don't want to come on too strong," he told Rex. "This is just a friendly chat."

Jen could hardly believe the squalor as they approached the trailer where the Grunwalds lived. Clutter covered the yard—broken tools, flat tires, and scraps of baling wire. Three or four cackling chickens strutted through the overflow of a trash pile that should have been disposed of long ago and whose remains were now scattered about like refuse at the county dump. The odor turned Jen's stomach. Struck by the sight, she moved slightly ahead of the group, lost in her search for Clara amid the wreckage. She remembered passing this place before while she was growing up and some branch of the Muncie family lived here. She didn't remember anything like this. The house was a ways from town and off the beaten track but not *that* isolated. Maybe people needed to be more concerned about their neighbors.

Before Jen's father and the others made it to the trailer, Luther Grunwald had met them in the yard, and when Jen joined them, they were standing by one of several junkers; torn-up cars and engines of various models littered the yard along with all the other refuse. There was even a small horse trailer among the rusting skeletons. Still keeping one eye out for young Clara, Jennifer listened as Mike Castle took charge of the conversation. Jen was wary of Luther, who was raw and grizzled but stronger than he appeared from a distance.

"You make any money off these junk heaps, Luther?" Sheriff Castle was asking.

"Oh, a little bit," said Grunwald, rubbing his bristled jaw. "Folks need parts here and there."

"How'd you come by 'em?" asked Castle evenly.

"Folks bring 'em by, lookin' to be rid of 'em. I take 'em off their hands. Most of 'em is old, as you can see. Been sittin' in someone's backyard ten years. Sometimes guys want twenty bucks; sometimes I get 'em free just for taking 'em off their hands. I sell a hub cap here, a spark plug there. It usually evens up. Sometimes I clear a little."

"What about that horse trailer?" Castle pressed. "It's seen better days, but who'd want to just go and leave it?"

They walked toward it, a fifth-wheel trailer meant for a single animal. Its sides were dented, and the paint that once made the outfit parade-ready silver with a decorative blue strip was peeling now into flecks of metallic dust. The words *Salt Desert Stampede* were printed in silver across the strip. Someone had scratched a large *X* after the word *stampede*. "Probably with a corkscrew," Castle said to Brodie, running his fingers along the lines of vandalism.

"A fellow down in Cedar Fort brought that in a year ago to have a hitch put on it," Grunwald explained. "I done the job, and then he couldn't pay me, which happens a lot these days. I ended up squarin' things by keepin' the trailer and giving him an old junk Ford I had here on the lot. Wasn't worth nuthin' to me, but it did run good enough to get the fellow back to Cedar Fort and leave me with his horse trailer free and clear. Don't know what I'll do with it. I got no horse. Probably sell it if the right price comes along."

"You pay your rent to Bill Muncie with any of these cars?" pressed the sheriff, no longer interested in the trailer.

Grunwald paused, suddenly alert. "What d'ya mean? If Muncie wants one of these old junkers, I guess he can have it."

"Muncie got picked up over by Wendover driving on stolen tags the other day. Claimed he got the car from here."

Grunwald threw his hands up mockingly. "Hah! You nabbed me, Sheriff. Arrest me for helpin' out a friend." Then he laughed mawkishly. "Hey, how do I know what comes in here? Some fella leaves a car one day last winter, and I never see hide nor hair of him again. Then last week, Muncie comes along, says he needs to borrow some wheels, and drives the car away. It's nothing to do with me."

"No, I suppose not," said Castle, still eyeing Grunwald up and down. Dill paced nervously beside him. Jen could tell he was anxious to do something, but this was Castle's ball game. Bishop Brodie merely looked about with complete restraint. He had been introduced to Grunwald, but the man obviously had no special regard for a Mormon bishop. Still, when Castle paused, Brodie took advantage of the opening.

"You've got a sweet little girl who's come to our church a time or two, Mr. Grunwald. My daughter here is her teacher in the Primary class. 'Clara,' I believe you call her. Jen would surely like to see her if she's around."

Luther barely acknowledged Jennifer. "I ain't a member of your church," he drawled at Brodie. "Clara's mama was before she passed away, and I think the girl is on your rolls. She don't come too often, but once in a while I drop her off on Sundays. Her mama was from up in Box Elder County. That's where her people live and where she's buried now."

"How long's your wife been gone?" asked Rex sympathetically.

"Close to two years," said Grunwald without expression. "Car wreck up in Brigham City. Now there's just me and the girl."

"It's got to be tough, raising a child on your own."

"We get by," Grunwald answered warily.

"So you never took a name from the fella that left the Plymouth here last winter," said Castle, still thinking of the stolen tags, "the one Muncie borrowed off your lot?"

"I mighta wrote it down somewhere, but I'd have to pay the devil to find it now," replied Grunwald. "Muncie's got his nerve sendin' you in my direction."

At this point, Clara appeared, poking her little scarecrow face around the beam that held up the corner of the trailer porch, a rickety affair that Jen feared a slight wind would obliterate. The attention of everyone turned to the girl, and Jennifer hurried toward her, wishing she could take her in her arms. "Clara!" she called. "Remember me? Your Primary teacher, Sister Brodie. I've come to see you. How are you today?"

Clara wore the same faded rose-print dress she'd had on at Primary, and she clutched the same one-eyed rag doll in her arm. Her hair stood out like wild straw; her eyes were piercing little pinholes of light, surveying Jennifer without blinking. Her brows remained pinched together in an angry scowl, but she didn't back away when Jen approached and seemed to accept her greeting with some level of curiosity. She jerked her hand out of reach, however, when Jen attempted to touch her, and Jen had to content herself with a simple conversation, hoping the girl would invite her in the house.

"So this is where you live," Jen said smiling. "Now that I know, I can wave as I pass by."

Clara looked steadfastly at Jennifer, but her expression did not change.

"There's your pretty doll," said Jennifer, stooping down. "Are there more in the house like her?"

Clara tightened her grip on the doll and backed up a step or two, suddenly mistrusting the Primary lady even more acutely.

Bishop Brodie walked up behind Jennifer and tipped his hat at the little girl. "Howdy, muffin."

Jen stood and took her father's arm. "This is *my* daddy, Clara. His name is Bishop Brodie. He's a leader at church." Suddenly, Jen looked at her dad and laughed. "But don't let that scare you," she told Clara. "He used to bounce me on his knee when I was a kid like you."

"You bet I did," said Brodie, "and I think Jen had a dolly just like that one, only maybe not as pretty, now that I recall."

Little Clara seemed almost ready to stop frowning when they were interrupted by a shout from Castle. "Come on out here, Brodie. I want you to take a look at this."

All of them followed a pathway to the far edge of the yard, beyond the barn, where a fringe of stubble rimmed the fence line and the desert stretched endlessly into the western horizon. Dill, looking handsome and official in his crisp new deputy's shirt and badge, winked at Jennifer but kept his distance, trying to remain professional as he followed Castle's lead. A pile of boulders dominated one side of the setting, some distance from the Muncie property line. Trailing down from its apex were more rocks and thistles until the ground leveled off to sand and eventually the grass and gravel that made up the Muncie land. Just over the property line, Castle drew Grunwald's attention to what looked like a small hole bored into the sand between some boards wedged there for designation. A red flag hung from a drooping rope strung haphazardly nearby, and the words *Danger: Keep Away* were painted on a plank that lay face down in the thistles.

"You've got a mine shaft here, Grunwald," said Sheriff Castle, poking in the sand hole with a stick and watching it cave in on all sides until the opening widened to the size of a cellar door. "Heaven knows how deep she is," Castle added, peering down the hole.

"You'll have to talk to Muncie about that," spit Grunwald. "This here's his place, not mine. I'm just a renter."

"Well, that's true," replied Castle, still poking about at the lip of the shaft. "But these things are a hazard the county's trying to eliminate. I would think you'd want to plug it up yourself, what with your little girl around. A kid could fall in there real easy."

"Clara don't come out here," said Grunwald. "She stays close to home."

"You never know about kids." Castle shrugged. "They can get away before you know it, and this hole ain't that far away from the house."

"She don't come out here, I'm tellin' ya. Nobody does. I've pitched some tumbleweeds in there now and again, but it's just a hole. Muncie can fill it up if he wants to pay for the shovel."

Castle tossed a stone into the pit and listened for a sound. When no one heard anything, Dill got down on his stomach and aimed a flashlight in the hole. "I can't see much," he said. "Just a bunch of weeds or something way down, almost out of sight. It's deep, I'll tell you that."

Sheriff Castle looked at little Clara standing several feet behind them with her doll. Then he turned to Grunwald with anger in his voice. "We're not waitin' for Muncie to pay for the shovel. The county will be comin' as soon as I can get 'em down here to fill up that shaft. In the meantime, I want a fence around that hole and that sign and flag as backup. You got that, Luther?" He stomped away, with one more disgusted glance at the Grunwald yard. "I'm checking up on you tomorrow," he called as he moved toward the car. "If that fence isn't there, I'll write you up for child endangerment, that's what I'll do."

Grunwald shrugged, toeing the ground, his hands jammed carelessly in his pockets. He avoided the sheriff's eyes. Car doors slammed and engines started, and Castle shook his finger a final time. "You get workin' on that fence!"

As Jennifer and her father drove away, she looked back at little Clara standing alone in that trash heap of a yard, clutching her doll and watching them go, her eyes never leaving the Brodie car. She agreed that the mine shaft needed to be fenced, but she wondered if antagonizing Luther Grunwald was the wisest thing to do.

"Do you think Luther will put a fence around the mine shaft, Dad?" Jen asked as they traveled home.

"For Clara's sake, I hope so," said Brodie, "but it won't be because of Sheriff Castle's threats."

"He's not worried about getting arrested?"

"Something got that fella's back up a long time ago. It's hardened him against authority or any kind of rule or anyone telling him what to do."

"What does that to people?" Jen wanted to know. She was thinking of Clara, a child who already had anger in her eyes at six years old.

"Life," said her father. "Some people just let life get the best of them. Bad things happen. It's more than they can stand. Life. It's never easy, Jen."

As Jennifer thought more about it, she wished Sheriff Castle had let her father handle Luther Grunwald. Maybe the fence around the old mine shaft would have gone up sooner.

Maybe it wouldn't have been so easy for Grunwald to drop me in this hole if there had been a fence around it. But maybe

I'm lucky that the hole was handy, that it was easy to just drop me in, and that it was the first thing that came to his mind when he was trying to wrestle me quiet. He might have killed me otherwise. Right there where we were. Yeah, I guess I'm lucky there wasn't any fence. Yeah, I guess I'm lucky.

Chapter Four

JENNIFER CLERKED THE REST OF the week at Dudley's Desert Boutique in town, working her own shift and filling in for Loretta Dudley, who made a trip to Reno with her husband and returned full of new ideas about snake-skinned purses (fake, of course) and "authentic" Indian sand art made in China. "I couldn't afford it otherwise," said Loretta, "and neither could my customers."

Dill stopped in the store occasionally just to say hello, and the couple made it into Salt Lake on Friday, which was his one night off. The movie they saw was a romantic comedy about some college kids who were generally acting like fools at the frat house. It was broad, slapstick humor, but Jen could tell that Dillon was uncomfortable.

"So that's what it's like when you're away at school?" His arm was around her as they left the theater. "Lots of fun and games?"

"That was a silly movie, Dill," said Jen defensively. "It's hardly like that at BYU. Provo's the most buttoned-down place on the planet!"

"What? No parties?" He grinned, but the words were only half in jest.

"Well, I wouldn't say *that*," returned Jen merrily. She liked Dill, even loved him, but was never above subtly reminding him that he was not her only pleasure. They both had many goals to complete before eternal commitments could be considered. Her doubts about his depth of feeling made it harder. Especially on the front porch after two a.m. on a summer night, like Tony had joked about. The moon was big and round, and the sky like star-crusted ink. You didn't see that in the city, where lights obliterated the natural wonders. In the country, everything was down-to-earth and simple. You fell for a guy, and you acted like it. There was no subtlety, no games, no analyzing. But Jennifer was growing up and learning to look at real love as a lot more complicated. Nineteen was kind of the cusp of adulthood. You weren't quite there, but you had all these feelings pushing you. Golly, life was difficult and wonderful and crazy and miraculous all at once.

Was it you all along? Were you the one? Will I ever get to know? Right now, right this minute, are you wondering where I am? Oh, don't worry, Dill. I'm all right. I'm here. I'm still alive. You'll find me. Get my dad to help you. He'll know what to do.

Clara Grunwald didn't come to Primary on Sunday, and when Loretta Dudley gave Jennifer that Monday off for putting in so many extra shifts, she decided to go riding for the first time since coming home. Perhaps she'd go by the Grunwald place and wave at her strange little class member. She felt sorry for the girl, living farther from town and other children as she did. She wanted Clara to feel part of things at Primary. She felt the need to coax her back.

Second to her family and Dill, Applejack, her buckskin pony, was what Jen missed most about being away in Provo. Tony liked to tease Dill and tell him that the horse came before he did, and then her dad one-upped him by saying he thought Applejack even beat out the rest of the Brodies on Jen's reasons-to-be-homesick list. Jennifer denied the accusation, but she did admit to dreaming of "flying across the fields on Applejack" when the pressures of freshman composition got to be too much. The idea of coming home to horse and saddle was a tonic, even as BYU pushed her enthusiastically into the greater world.

After spending a glorious half hour rounding up her pony, Jennifer almost decided to skip the visit to the Grunwalds. Better to roam her own fields and trails where she could look out over the valley from familiar vantage points and salve the ache of homesickness that had lingered all year in Provo, despite the fun she'd had. Letting Applejack nuzzle Corn Flakes from her hand was a ritual she'd missed since Christmas. He was a sleek colt with white forelegs. He was her baby, her pride. His soft nose in her palm delighted her. His large, shining eyes, watching her every move, was like a familiar smile, reflecting her own. She bridled and saddled the horse and was soon trotting him around her mother's garden and through the raspberry patch, careful to keep to the designated paths.

"There's no race track through my raspberries," called Evelyn Brodie from the kitchen window. "Why don't you take him through the lower field to the canyon trail."

"I'm just getting comfortable," Jen yelled back. "It's been awhile."

Evelyn watched as her daughter took another leisurely loop around the vines. Then Jen found her way to a fresh route along a tree line to the west. She picked up speed as the path widened and the pony found its pace. Jennifer's blonde hair, partly trimmed by a nestled braid, bounced off her back, and her sun hat slid down her shoulder, held only by its strap.

Evelyn smiled and turned back to her dishes. It was good
to have Jen home again. She wondered if Dudley's was the
best place for Jennifer to spend her time that summer. Rex
was right. Jen had so much potential as a teacher or some
other social professional. Perhaps she should have taken
some semester abroad program or some health aid project
opportunity in Africa. Evelyn winced a little and felt guilty.
The truth was she had selfishly discouraged anything like
that, at least for now. "Come home this year," she'd told Jen
in the spring. "I've missed you so much. It's been so hard
to have you gone. Come home one more summer. Then
we'll see. Besides, Dill will be here until August. You'll want
to spend some time with him before he goes." Evelyn was
hoping Jen would come home for Dillon Dancie, if not for
her. And her reasoning seemed to do the trick.

If I don't make it out of here, I hope my mother never realizes
I didn't die right off. I hope she never knows I suffered, or even
thinks it. I couldn't bear to hurt her. She loves me so.

Jennifer and Applejack had covered a good five miles
before they turned for home. Good riding trails were
plentiful, and horse and rider could be alone and enjoy the
solitude Jen cherished. She loved the broad expanse of sky
and the flat vistas of her desert home. Sure, parts of it were
barren and thirsty-looking—a panorama of sagebrush and
sand stretching as far as anyone could see—but add a little
water, and you get green fields and her mother's raspberry
vines. Add a mountain here or there, and you get a sunset
that would take your breath away. Add a mom and dad
like hers, and even a mouthy younger brother, and you
get a family worth coming home to, folks who had made
something of the land. Jennifer liked thinking these things
every now and then, and sometimes it took a lonely ride on
Applejack to do it.

She rode a good distance then swung around at the back of Grunwald's place sort of as an afterthought. Getting caught up in the reverie of being home again had led her to almost forget about little Clara. But she decided to make the stop, worried about the girl who hadn't come back to Primary and hoping Luther had put up that fence around the mine shaft.

Approaching from the back side of the property, Jennifer was still a quarter mile off, but she could tell that nothing much had changed. She slowly trotted closer, hoping to avoid any confrontation. The rope and red flag dangled listlessly near the pit, as they had before. There was no fence. It looked the same as it had a week before, at least from forty yards away. So did the trash heap between the tree line and the trailer, and Grunwald's jalopies still stood as iron skeletons from another era, moldering in the dust.

Jennifer did notice an extra pickup parked next to Grunwald's rust heap near the barn, a green GMC with an extended cab that was in better condition that anything else on the premises. Vaguely wondering whether Luther's clientele was improving, she reined a shuddering Applejack up to the trailer and dismounted, hoping Clara would see her and come out. She didn't particularly want to face Luther Grunwald, though she was determined to speak to him for Clara's sake if necessary. For a while everything was quiet except the cackling of the chickens, and then Clara did appear, gnome-like and impish, peeking around the corner of the trailer door with her angular pinched face and bulging eyes.

"Clara!" cried Jen, smiling. "There you are!"

The little girl, holding her doll, opened the door a little wider. She seemed astonished and intimidated by the horse.

"This is Applejack," said Jen, noticing her interest. "We decided to come and see you, so I'm glad you're home."

The horse tossed its head and whinnied, and Jen looked at Clara, expecting a smile, but the girl only stared, somewhat overwhelmed. "I've had Applejack since he was born," Jen told her. "I saw him when he was just a baby, lying by his mother in the straw. He's called a buckskin horse. That's because he's kind of leather-colored. Do you see that? But he's also got these white forelegs, which are pretty special."

Jennifer kept patting Applejack and trying to think of what to say to Clara, who, of course, never replied to anything. Presently, the little girl sat down on the trailer porch and put her chin between her knees, as if Jen wasn't there. She still clutched the same rag doll and wore the same dress, and now she was reverting to the same intensely blank expression.

"Here, let me show you how it's done," said Jennifer, suddenly struck with an idea. Moving to the pony's side, she climbed quickly into the saddle. "Come on, Apple. Good boy," she said, reining the obedient animal in a circle about the yard, burying her face in his flowing mane at one point and throwing her arms around his neck in gratitude when she was finished. "Oh, what a fine pony you are!" she told him as she jumped down. Even this raised no smile from Clara, but she did clap her hands together when Jen returned to the porch.

"Would you like to go for a ride?" Jennifer asked suddenly. "I could take you in the saddle with me, no problem at all. I'd hold on tight, and Apple's very gentle. I promise."

Clara nodded her head eagerly, and a flicker of a smile crossed her face, and then Jen paused, realizing that she might have spoken up too soon. "Uh . . . we better ask your daddy first. Is he around?"

Without hesitation, and for the first time since she'd known the child, Clara Grunwald reached out and took

Jen's hand. No coaxing, no persuading, no wishing it would happen for teacher-student bonding purposes. Clara was pulling her toward the sloping barn where her father was obviously occupied and where she could obtain permission for the ride on Applejack. Jennifer gratefully let herself be led. She was glad the girl wanted something from her, happy to be a source of pleasure for this strange little creature who had so few of life's rewards.

They trudged past the rusted truck and the unfamiliar GMC and then entered a shadowy, straw-strewn shed that could have once been a working stable. There were stalls and a feeding trough on one side, under the eaves and the remnants of a sinking roof. No animals were in sight, and several bales of rotted hay appeared to hold up the corners of the barn. There was a separate room at the far end, and Clara seemed to be headed in that direction when she suddenly stopped and pointed at the door. It was halfway open, and Jennifer could hear voices from inside and see Luther from behind. She couldn't tell what was being said, but it didn't seem like a private conversation. The door wasn't even closed.

Letting go of Clara's hand, she confidently marched forward, thinking Luther might be more polite with company around. And that's when it happened. Suddenly. Before she had any time to think. She was standing in the doorway of some kind of shabby office when Grunwald's gun went off, and she was too shocked to move when she saw Bill Muncie's body lurch toward her, all 225 pounds of him, as the swivel chair he fell against went crashing to the floor.

Chapter Five

THAT BACKSTABBER BILL MUNCIE! IT was all *his* fault! So reasoned a frustrated, smarting Luther Grunwald as he traipsed across his yard that morning, returning from the pit. He cursed his luck. He hadn't meant to shoot Bill Muncie. That's why he'd dropped the gun as soon as it went off. It clattered on the stone floor just as Muncie did after he hit that chair. Luther couldn't believe what he'd done. He'd pulled that trigger before he even realized it. And then the girl was there, as startled as he was, looking from him to Muncie and back again like she'd just laid eyes on the devil! Well, in a way, that's exactly what she'd done. Muncie was a lyin' cheat, and he got what he had comin'! Luther himself hadn't asked for any of it, and he'd fight tooth and nail before anyone would make him pay!

As these thoughts raced through his mind, Grunwald stopped walking and made an effort to gain some control. Everything had happened quickly—the killing of Bill Muncie, the disposing of this girl. Now he needed time to think. He looked down for a moment at his hands and noticed his right index finger, red and punctured and swelling. "Dang girl bit me!" he murmured, and then he caught the color of two golden strands of hair twisted around the same finger, and he remembered the girl's long tresses and how some of her hair had fallen this way and that as she wrestled with him. Luther gritted his teeth. The reality of what he'd done began to settle heavily on him. His eyes darted about the squalid yard, searching for some way to cope with his problems, all the while reviewing his options.

Once more he pondered the fragile strands of hair still wrapped around his finger. Gently he rubbed his thumb against them. Finally he circled them carefully around a button on his shirt. A plan was springing to life in his mind, and with it came determination. He allowed his eyes to wander one more time to where the obscure old mine shaft held a terrible secret, and then he set his efforts to the vital business at hand. Making quick work of his first inclination, he picked up a five-foot plank lying in the yard, slung it under his arm, and stooped to lift another of the same length nearby. He found two more pieces of wood and retraced his steps. Soon all four boards lay across the mouth of the pit. He tore the rope and red flag down. No use calling attention to the mine shaft anymore. A fence wasn't called for either. There were gaps between the planks. They weren't a perfect fit, but Grunwald was satisfied. The mouth of the pit was covered well enough. It would even sit well with the county sheriff, Luther figured, if he ever came by again.

Quickly and methodically, Grunwald positioned Muncie's green pickup in front of the horse trailer at the far end of the yard. The little two-wheeled, silver cart had been gathering mud and rust since before Luther and Clara moved in the year before. Luther took a moment to chuckle to himself over the story he'd told Mike Castle about getting the horse trailer from a guy who couldn't pay his bill. He was good at those quick little spur-of-the-moment lies. Always had been. He didn't really know where the trailer had come from, and he didn't care. It would serve his purpose now. It was covered, had adequate tires, and would work for what he needed. He knew he had to get rid of the pony as soon as possible, and this trailer was a godsend. Muncie and his GMC must disappear as well, and now all three could be taken care of in one fell swoop. The desert was a huge, lonely swath of God's great earth. Grunwald intended to make the most of it.

Grunwald wondered briefly about Clara as he attached the horse trailer to the hitch, but she didn't worry him. He knew she was probably staring bug-eyed from the little window in her bedroom, where she liked to hide. He'd lock her in before he left, but he doubted she'd leave the trailer even if he didn't. They were three miles from town and a mile off the paved highway. The nearest neighbor was in sight, but too far for a six-year-old to walk, even if she wanted to, which she didn't. Clara was a homebody. She usually spent her time in the trailer watching cartoons on a dim old Motorola or lurking around the edges of the property, clutching her moth-eaten doll and gazing out at the world with her bulbous eyes, waiting for the sky to fall in or who knew what. No, Luther wasn't worried about Clara taking off and telling anybody anything. There wasn't anywhere for her to go and nothing for her to tell since she didn't speak or write or even nod. Besides, he wasn't sure how much Clara had even seen, hightailing it like she did. She'd been known to hide away after a scolding and not appear again until hunger began to gnaw or a cold wind came up.

His eyes swept the yard as he untied the horse from the porch post and led it to where he'd positioned the trailer near the barn. He wondered if the blonde girl had told anyone she was coming here or if anyone had seen her heading this direction. He was gambling otherwise. He knew he had the advantage of being off any main crossing. Their place was a mile from the highway, down a lightly traveled dirt road, and back in a corner. You had to kind of know where you were going to find the place. He liked it that way.

Grunwald couldn't help admiring the buckskin's trappings as he maneuvered the animal into the trailer. There was a nice Indian blanket underneath the saddle and silver conchos on leather strips trimming the stirrups. The back of the saddle was etched with some kind of artistic engraving or pattern. It wasn't cheap. "Rich ranchers!" he murmured, slapping the horse's rump. The animal slid obediently into the trailer, tossing its head and snorting, its dark eyes looking vainly for its rider.

Within minutes, Grunwald had wrapped Bill Muncie's body in a frayed carpet and dragged it out of the barn and next to the horse's tenuous hooves in the trailer. There was plenty of room for both the horse and the man, wrapped as he was, and the journey would not last long. He made one more careful survey of the barn and vicinity, assuring himself that no other hint of either Muncie or the girl remained. He packed the pistol with him, the one he'd used to kill his landlord not an hour before, and then he slowly settled into the driver's seat of the pickup to follow a deserted, dusty road into the desert.

About ten miles along a line of scrub oak at the bottom of a sandy gully, Grunwald pulled to a stop and got out to look around. Finding that he was alone and that isolation stretched as far as he could see, he opened the trailer and released the horse, nudging him down the tipped gate of the cart and sending him on his way with a whoop and holler. When the pretty pony lingered, tossing its head and looking curiously back at the truck and trailer, Grunwald yelled louder and pelted the horse with pebbles until one of them stung its rump. The buckskin jerked away, finally galloping back in the direction of the town.

Grunwald watched him go, taking a moment to wipe the sweat off with his hat. Then he returned to the truck and drove five miles farther down the gully, exiting where the pathway flattened and lost itself in the rocks and sagebrush near the foothills on the south. There he removed Muncie's body from the trailer, still rolled in the carpet, and unhooked the trailer from the truck. He purposely positioned the cart and sent it rolling off a high ledge, where it bounced like a toy into a ravine and landed on its side, scraped and dented, and covered by the brush above it. Unless you stood at an exact angle or knew what you were looking for, the wreckage was hard to see, which pleased Grunwald immensely. Nevertheless, he took the time to hike into the little canyon and cover the trailer with sand and greasewood and whatever foliage he could find.

The climb back to the top was arduous, and Grunwald sat in the cab of the GMC and rested for several minutes after he arrived. He stared silently through the windshield at the barren desert around him, his eyes dull and lightless. Finally, he moved to finish his work, thoughtlessly, mechanically, as if he were in a trance. He unwrapped Bill Muncie's body from the carpet and lifted the dead man into the passenger side of the truck, leaving the man facing the windshield, leaning over the dashboard, and still wearing his hat. The next moment, Luther was in the driver's seat, apparently not the least bit bothered by his grotesque traveling companion.

He made his way back toward his place, following a zigzag pattern as he drove for about three miles. When an overhang of rocks appeared, the shadow of a smile crossed his face, and he lost no time completing his entire plan. He parked the truck and, after a bit of awkward lifting and pushing, got Muncie into the driver's seat underneath the steering wheel. Then he wiped his own prints from every inch of space— the wheel, the gear shift, the dash, anything he touched, including the pistol he placed near Muncie's hand, which hung limply across the console. The man had been hit in the chest, probably in the heart, Grunwald surmised, since death came so suddenly. It wasn't a typical suicide shot, but it would do.

Grunwald stood and pondered Muncie for a moment. Again he cursed and then turned and spit into the sand. Muncie was to blame here. None of this ever needed to happen, and it wasn't *his* fault that it did. He was always cleaning up for the stupidity of those around him. This had been a bad one, maybe the worst ever. But it looked like with a little luck, he'd get home free.

Carefully, he unwound the two strands of blonde hair from the button on his shirt. Ejecting a CD from the pickup's player, he laid the hair just inside the slit so that the strand caught at the corner when the CD was replaced. He could see it easily without really searching for it, and he knew a crime tech would have no trouble finding it at all. Luther looked at the CD and chuckled. It was "I'd Die for You" by the Spinners. Even he could see the irony in that!

Once more, Luther Grunwald wiped away any trace of his presence at the scene. Satisfied, he walked the remaining five miles back to his squalid oasis in the trees, making sure to hide his tracks as he moved. He'd brought some bottled water with him and took his time, having no trouble with the distance.

It was still light when he arrived. Clara had not seen fit to turn the lamp on in the trailer yet, but he was sure she was there because he'd locked the door. She was probably glued to the television set, he decided, quickly forgiving himself for leaving her alone all day. Yeah, she'd had the TV tuned to some kid show and probably didn't even know or care that he was gone. Television. What a waste. He didn't let her watch the bad stuff on TV. You couldn't trust the media these days.

He went in and found the girl where he thought she'd be, curled up with her doll on the sagging sofa opposite the dining table, which sat four when it wasn't folded down. The TV rested on top, its rabbit-ear antenna making a V shape against the back window. The television was on, but the volume was muted. Clara had fallen asleep, probably while eating Pop Tarts, pieces of which lay in crumbles on the couch. Luther paused to cover her with a nearby blanket. Then he dropped into the nearest chair and removed his hat. After his long walk and the stress he'd just experienced, it felt good to ease back, close his eyes, and relax, even as he congratulated himself for his accomplishment.

He never remembered actually sleeping, but he must have drifted off, for when Clara nudged him awake, it was dark. He could tell she was hungry, so he opened a can of soup and heated it on the stove, ladling it out with some crackers for the two of them. "Anyone come around here today while I was gone?" he said to the little girl. "Anyone asking questions?" Clara slurped her soup and eyed him dubiously.

They watched television for a while after dinner, but Clara soon grew bored with the noisy wrestling match Luther preferred and disappeared into her bedroom in the back of the trailer. When he checked on her later, he found her playing quietly with her doll and drawing crayon pictures on a cardboard box.

He had trouble keeping his mind on the TV set as well and finally set about searching the trailer and then the barn for a high-power lantern he thought he had somewhere. He never found it and had to settle for the long flashlight hanging by a leather strap in the trailer closet. Its batteries were low, and he kicked himself for being so unprepared as to not have a thing so simple as a flashlight. But who knew *this* was going to happen?

Still, his plans had gone quite well. A couple of times that evening he had determined he would put his thoughts aside, go to bed, and let tomorrow come. But for all the day's success, one thing nagged at him, and when he was certain Clara was sound asleep, he left the trailer and made his way beyond the edge of the yard where the mouth of the mine shaft lay hidden in the darkness beneath the planks. Kicking the boards away, he aimed his light into the hole and watched the beam bounce from side to side as he found the proper bearing. All was quiet, save the sound of a nearby cricket and of a light wind ruffling the desert sage. He lay down on his stomach and aimed the light into the shaft, following it with his eyes and listening for any movement. "You down there, girl?" he called, muffling his voice in the cup of his hand out of false caution—no one was close enough to hear. "Did the fall do you in, or are you still breathin'?"

Grunwald paused, waiting for some response. The shaft offered only silence. A vertical aim of the flashlight beam showed nothing of any significance, at least as far as the glow extended—only a tangle of weeds and branches that he could barely see in the dimming light. The pit was deep. Even deeper than he had reckoned. "You shouldn't 'ave come nosin' around here like ya did," he called again into the dark eye of the shaft. "You stumbled on a scene that wasn't yours to witness. And now you're dead for all I know. If you're not, you better start to holler 'cause there's no way out of there without a lot of help." Again, Luther waited, and again he was met with only silence from the hole. Finally rising to his feet, he shoved the long planks back in place, brushed the sand off his shirt, and turned back toward the trailer, letting his flashlight guide him home.

Chapter Six

IT WAS SEVERAL HOURS BEFORE anyone at the Brodie house realized Jennifer was missing. When Applejack trotted into the back alfalfa field, his bit askew, his flanks and fetlocks covered with sand, Evelyn had just arrived home from a day in Tooele. After she'd waved at Jen from the kitchen window that morning, she'd hurried to ready herself for a trip to town. There was a stake Relief Society meeting at eleven, a stop at Sullivan's Music for some piano pieces the ward had ordered, grocery shopping, and a visit with Grandma Bentley at the care center in Stansbury Park. She had left chops on the drain board, thawing for dinner. Expecting to be running late, she had asked Jennifer to put them in the oven if she wasn't home by four. Coming in at almost four thirty, she was surprised to find the meat still wrapped and untouched.

Tony had had baseball practice that morning. He played for a city league once the school year ended, and he squeezed in a summer job at his father's implement business in the afternoons. The games were at night, under the lights at the city park, and mornings were ideal for practice, especially in mid-July when it was still cool enough to breathe. The coach was getting the boys used to the regimen now, said Tony, and they would appreciate it later. He'd left the house before Jen got up that morning and hadn't been home all day.

Along with his father and three brothers, Rex Brodie had once run several hundred head of cattle on his family's land in the south part of the county. But family ranching was in some ways a dying occupation, so Rex had sold most of his holdings off some years before and now maintained a successful business selling agricultural equipment. He still had an acreage, a few animals, and a hay field. He liked to think his soul was in both places—the city and the country— partly for his own protection and love of the land.

He was a strong man physically, tall and broad-shouldered, but his heart was tender, especially when it came to those he cared for. It was one reason he gave up ranching. His ward members lived many lives in many places, and he wanted his heart to be wherever they were, understanding their needs. That Monday, the bishop was spending his time like he did most other days—chatting with customers, selling his combines and tractors and machinery, and thinking. Always thinking about his ward and his own family—Tony's ball games, Jenny's summer romance with Dill Dancie. Bishop Brodie's heart was in his work that Monday, both the city and the country side of things. A "bishop's heart," Evelyn called it. "A father's heart is what I always want to have at home," he told her. He was unaware that both kinds were about to break.

"Hey," said Tony, as he and his father turned into the yard at five, "isn't that Apple out in the south field?" He pointed to the horse, fifty yards away, walking gingerly through the furrows and clods of the newly plowed ground. "What's he doing out there?"

"I dunno," said Rex, shading his eyes and squinting in that direction.

He stuck his head in the back door and called through the archway to the kitchen. "Evelyn, is Jennifer in there?" When he got no answer, he went in and met his wife coming toward him, wiping her hands on her apron.

"Is Jen around?" he asked. "How come she left Apple in the furrows?"

"What? Apple's in the furrows? What are you talking about?"

Tony had already made his way around his mother's garden and raspberry patch and skirted the grass until he arrived directly across from where the buckskin pony stood. Then he trudged through the uneven furrows to the horse's side, calming him with familiar pats and whispers. Inspecting the animal and the gear made the boy anxious, and he wasted no time picking up the dragging lines and leading Apple home.

I wonder what Grunwald did with Applejack. Did he just turn him loose and send him home? Good pony, Apple. Too bad he's not a dog. A dog could sniff around and find me. A dog would run right back here and show everybody where I am. I love you, Apple, but right now, I wish you were a dog.

"Where is Jen?" said Evelyn, untroubled but curious when she glimpsed the pony. "You wouldn't think she'd leave him out there, saddled like that. Why didn't she bring him in?" Evelyn was never one to imagine catastrophe. She'd arrived home half an hour earlier, found Jennifer not home, and simply gone to work preparing dinner. The chops were in the oven. She was tossing a salad. "I called her cell," she explained to her husband, "but it's on the kitchen counter. The thing rang right under my ear almost! Scared me to death! Then I remembered she left it here when she took Apple out this morning."

Evelyn suddenly stopped and looked at Rex. "Wait a minute. Surely Jen hasn't been gone all day without her phone. That's not like her. And why would she go and leave the horse wandering around like that?"

Suddenly Evelyn turned pale. Her fingers gripped her husband's arm, and there was terror in her eyes. She began to stumble off the back steps, her gaze riveted on Tony bringing Applejack through the gate. "Oh my heavens!"

Rex rushed to the pair. Apple's hide was covered with sand and stickers. His mane was tangled, his tail slimed. Jennifer's saddle and trappings were scratched, dusty, and fouled by some kind of sap. The saddle hung loosely on the horse's back; the blanket was dragging. The proud animal tossed its head and moved unhappily as Tony held the lines and tried to steady him. Rex patted Apple's neck and whispered soft words in his ears, and the horse stepped gingerly in a circle, but what they needed to know, Apple couldn't tell them. Everything was amiss. The order of their lives had suddenly been violently shoved out of balance. They searched each other's eyes but found no answers there.

While Tony took care of Applejack, Evelyn and Rex drove every lane and road that looped their place. Then Rex gassed up the Ditch Devil, an ATV made for water-master duties, and explored the smaller trails that snaked in and out along the fences and canals of his own pastures and those of several neighbors. Evelyn got on the telephone and, partly out of sheer frustration, called every friend and relative she knew. She made an effort to remain calm, especially at first, but ended up in tears when the answers were all the same:

"No, I haven't seen Jen today."

"She was supposed to call this afternoon, but I've never heard a word. Is something wrong?"

"What do you mean you can't find Jenny?"

Rex knifed into the desert, beyond the line where anything was claimed or cultivated. The little Devil roared through the sand on its knobby wheels and whipped up a cloud at its tail, but there was no sign of Jennifer. The sun was dropping out of sight when Bishop Brodie headed home, avoiding his wife's anguished glances, dreading the next call he would have to make.

"Surely there's an explanation." Evelyn's face twisted in denial. She shook her head, looking to her husband for an answer she knew he couldn't give. "Surely this isn't . . . oh, Rex," she was trembling, "not Jenny!"

By Tuesday morning, word of Jennifer Brodie's disappearance had traveled through the valley, and every law enforcement officer between Wendover and Salt Lake was on alert. Local authorities were peppered with the usual questions. Were they sure this wasn't just a young woman leaving home? The girl was nearly twenty and legally an adult. She could come and go as she pleased. Who was to say she hadn't had some kind of quarrel with her boyfriend or her parents and had just taken off to Las Vegas or Salt Lake? Maybe she went back to Provo, where her college friends all were. Calls were made, past residences checked.

But everyone close to Jen already knew she was no runaway. There had been no quarrel, no reason for her to disappear. Over the next three days, neighbors, ward members, and volunteers searched every inch of ground for three miles around the Brodie place, walking hand-to-hand in long lines so as not to miss anything. Anyone who may have seen Jennifer on Monday was immediately questioned, and that was a time-consuming chore, since Sheriff Castle had to leave Dillon Dancie out of the investigation; the kid was useless.

"He's a wreck," Castle told Rex Brodie. "*You* have the right to fall apart on me. Not him."

"No one's falling apart," said Brodie, who seemed to age each time Castle talked to him. "We're all standing tall for Jenny. But we need some answers, Mike. Every hour that goes by twists the knife in a little deeper. You can understand that. You got to give me something I can tell Evelyn. Anything. She's a mother, and there's only so much she can take."

"Yeah, and you're a father, aren't you, Rex?" said Castle softly. "It works both ways." He put a sympathetic hand on the bishop's shoulder, and both men sensed that their usual roles of giver and receiver had been reversed. Castle was the "authority" now, the man who had the temporal power to get things done. And the Brodies desperately needed all that he could give them—and the grace of God as well.

Castle went to see Luther Grunwald. He had no suspicions. The Grunwald place was just the last of a string of stops he made, though he was aware that Jennifer knew little Clara through church. Grunwald was puttering in his yard when the sheriff stopped, and Castle cast one eye in the direction of the mine shaft as he approached. It was still not fenced, but Castle had other things concerning him at present.

"How ya doin', Luther?" he began, hoping for simple cooperation.

Grunwald continued his tinkering without looking up. "Sheriff."

"I see you ain't got that shaft fenced off yet, like you promised. When's that gonna happen?"

Grunwald stopped and looked over Castle's shoulder at the distant pit. "I slung some planks across the hole," he said. "If you want a fence, you'll have to talk to Muncie."

"When I talk to Muncie, I'll be tellin' him about the backhoe I ordered that's comin' to fill up that hole," declared Castle staunchly. He was tired of Grunwald and his attitude, and Muncie, too, for that matter.

Grunwald shrugged indifferently and returned to the carburetor he was cleaning.

"What I really came for was to ask you about a young woman that's missing. It's Jennifer Brodie, the bishop's girl, the one that was here the other day talking to that little one of yours. Her horse came home without her Monday afternoon, and no one's seen hide nor hair of her all night or all day today. Her folks are worried, of course. Her mother's dang near lost her mind. Everyone's scouring the desert. I'm just out asking if anyone saw the girl sometime yesterday."

Grunwald paused again. "Riding her horse, you say?"

"Yeah, a buckskin pony with white feet."

"No, I can't say I saw her anywhere around here. I would have remembered, too, since I'd just seen her the other day." Grunwald shook his head and turned away. "No, she wasn't here."

"What about the little girl?" pressed Castle. "Maybe she saw something."

"Clara? She never saw nothing."

"Could I talk to her?"

"She couldn't tell ya nothing. She's dumb, ya know."

At that moment Clara stuck her head out of the trailer door. Luther, seeing her, called out, "Hey, muffin, the sheriff wants to know if you saw that Brodie gal yesterday, your teacher at the church. He's looking for her. Shake your head if she was here."

The little girl stared out at Castle, her brows pinched together in her usual scowl. She remained as silent as a stone.

"The young lady would have been riding a horse with white feet," Sheriff Castle told the child hopefully, but Clara continued to be unresponsive. Her round, wide-set eyes—curious eyes—stared out at the world. Castle left, not entirely satisfied. He had no real suspicions about Luther. But he did see Clara in a different light. She was "dumb" in one respect. Still, Castle wondered if there might be more intelligence behind those silent eyes than anybody knew.

Were there noises up above? Some kind of engine maybe? She wasn't sure. Everything was far away. The man, Grunwald, came in the night. She thought she heard his voice, but she'd been afraid to speak. Maybe she should have begged his help. Maybe she would if he came again. She was alive, and he could save her. But maybe it was better that he didn't know . . .

Chapter Seven

DEEP IN THE DARKNESS, JENNIFER Brodie squinted at the crease of light in the sliver of sun above her. Air seeped through that wedge, enough to keep her alive but not enough to scour the shaft of dust and the odor of the decades—discarded trash, bird droppings, and even dead animals. Jen tried to close her mind to everything around her but the light. She'd been in a daze, in and out of a dreamlike trance where reality was only an occasional visitor. Trying to move, she felt a jolt of pain so sharp she groaned against its touch. It was the second morning. The night had passed in an agonizing haze of terror and apprehension, punctuated by periods of unconsciousness.

The previous day was still a blur. She could hear the sound of Luther Grunwald's gun exploding in the barn. She could see Bill Muncie falling over the swivel chair and crashing to the floor. There was the memory of clawing and kicking, desperately trying to get out of Grunwald's grip, and then the drop into the pit. All of it brought panic surging back into her heart. The fall, so sudden and unexpected, had taken her breath away and nearly more than that. As her mind cleared, she remembered waking up deep in the tumbleweeds, upside down and bleeding. The tangled branches had scraped and scratched her skin unmercifully. Her hair was matted with blood. It was wet and sticky—she could feel it with her fingers when she tried to push the strands out of her eyes.

Once she was awake, she had spent the first half hour screaming, pausing only to pant and gather strength. Her heart thudded against her chest and tripped like a clock in her ears and temples until she thought the sound would drive her crazy, and all to no avail. No one else could hear the drumming. She had whimpered like a child and begged for her father to come. "Daddy," she had groaned. "Momma, I'm right here!" The darkness, thick and dry, was oppressive and conjured in her psyche a lifelong dread of graves. The mine shaft's sandy walls closed in with claustrophobic tightness, leaving her pinned from all directions by their measure. She fought the urge to feel defeated. She was not a child anymore. She was nearly twenty. She was a competent young woman. The year at BYU had taught her something about overcoming fear. She should at least give survival a try, she told herself during a lucid moment. She was her father's daughter, after all. There was no way a Brodie would give in to circumstance. But she was weak and injured and needed to fully clear her head. Then she'd figure something out. Was it that, she wondered, or had she simply lost the strength to scream? Later, she lay quiet, drained of energy and hope, ready to surrender to the pit.

All these various emotions alternated through her mind. In the darkness, hot tears fell silently from her eyes, coursing backward down the bottom of her cheeks, for she was in a precarious position—both literally and figuratively—and faces floated before her: her mother, Dad, and Tony; Dill, of course, with his sunny hair and yearning eyes; her Grandma

Bentley; all the friends who knew and loved her; the ward members; her Primary kids; even little Clara Grunwald, who was obviously also a victim here. She felt a swell of determination that suddenly consumed her. She prayed that it would be enough.

A bleeding injury should be kept elevated, she remembered from first aid class. She needed to right herself if only for that reason. Doing so was difficult. Moving her arm was painful—she suspected a broken or dislocated shoulder. Sometimes she could barely breathe, which made her wonder if she'd cracked a rib or worse. Twisting her body and moving vertically in the opposite direction not only sharpened her misery but sent her deeper into the creeping, tangled branches of the tumbleweeds, which almost covered her by the time she was upright. The once balloon-like bushes, standing five or six yards high from the bottom of the pit, had cushioned her descent, but they offered neither a soft pillow nor a firm foundation. Jennifer pushed her head upward through the sticky branches, and her body seemed to settle at a certain point without sinking any farther. At last she could see daylight at the shaft's mouth about fifty feet above her; she hoped the tumbleweeds would hold.

When darkness fell the first night and Luther came, aiming his flashlight down into the pit, Jennifer was still too dazed and frightened to respond. Later, when she was thinking more clearly, she considered remaining silent, pretending to be dead, until a friendly rescuer arrived. She thought about it long and hard, mulling every consequence. As the hours passed, she saw some advantage to another option. Her positive nature told her Grunwald hadn't really planned to throw her in the pit, and by now there was a possibility he regretted doing it. She'd seen him commit a terrible act, it was true, so at that moment he was probably frustrated and scared. It was an impulsive thing that he might be having second thoughts about and wishing he could change. Maybe shooting Muncie was an accident. There had been an argument. Things had happened way too fast and gotten out of hand. Grunwald threw her in the pit out of desperation. Now, racked with guilt, he would be relieved to find she had survived. All she had to do was wait until he came around again and then yell her head off, and he would gratefully pull her out. The only other hope was that someone else would do it, and so far, there wasn't anybody else. There was no one to hear her screams.

Jennifer toyed with the idea of Luther Grunwald saving her. It had a lot to recommend it. Until now, Grunwald hadn't seemed to be a wicked man. He had a daughter. He was someone she knew. Her father hadn't spoken ill of him. Of course, Jennifer had never heard her father speak an unkind word about anyone even *before* he was called to be a bishop. Maybe Luther Grunwald *was* a better man than he appeared and would redeem himself by rescuing her in the end.

Maybe. But she reluctantly cast the plan aside as too much of a risk. If Grunwald regretted his action, he was terribly slow in getting help. He hadn't been near the pit the second day. He hadn't come the first day either. Not until after dark. He'd chased her and knocked her down and done all he could to keep her from screaming anything about Bill Muncie being shot. He'd thrown her in a hole to keep her quiet. Was she going to bet her life that he'd suddenly had a change of heart?

So when darkness settled the first night and the pit turned black and Luther came at last with his flashlight, Jen was glad she hadn't had the strength to beg. If he came again, she vowed, she would sink as far as she could go into the tumbleweeds, tighten every muscle, and as painful as it was, try not to breathe. Who knew what the man would do if he realized she was still alive?

But on this, the second morning, Jen ached with a fresh surge of panic. She was cold and hungry and in pain. She had managed to fool Grunwald into thinking she was dead, but she was no closer to being rescued. The shaft was just as deep and as dark as it had ever been. No one knew where she was except the man who'd put her there and possibly a little girl who couldn't speak. How long could she last like this, with no water and no food? Though it was late May and warm as taffy under the western Utah sun, the pit was cold, especially at night. Jen shivered in her cotton shirt and jeans. Her shoulder continued to throb. There were places on her face and head that were badly bruised and tender to the touch. Deep scratches stung and burned.

She worked to smother her fear by arguing against every negative reality that had given rise to it. She *was* closer to being rescued, perhaps only hours or even minutes away, she told herself. Dill and her father had been looking for her since yesterday. She was sure of it. Why, several people were probably searching for her by now—Tony, her mother, maybe even Brother Andrews and Larry Wishborne, their home teachers. Someone must have seen her riding Apple down the road to the Grunwald place. Her dad would put two and two together and come here. Why, in no time at all, someone would be calling her name from the opening above. She'd have an exciting story to tell her friends. That was for sure! If it just wasn't so dirty and dark and cold.

As for food and water, she wasn't hungry yet. Not at all. Her stomach recoiled at the thought. She was beginning to feel weak, however, and couldn't remember when she'd eaten last. A banana for breakfast yesterday? She didn't know. She *was* thirsty. Really thirsty. There was no doubt of that, and there was sand in her mouth to boot. She spit out the grit and began sucking on a piece of tumbleweed just to gather some saliva and take her mind away from the water she didn't have. At the same time, she decided to take advantage of all the warmth she could gather while a glint of sun filtered in. In the meantime she would listen hard for any sound of someone other than Luther Grunwald in the yard or near the pit.

She thought of little Clara, an innocent child, and yet part of a violent act because she had probably seen it happen—or had at least become aware of what her father had done to Bill Muncie and Jen. In her tender heart, she hoped the girl had avoided seeing anything. She hoped in Clara's six-year-old mind it had all been just a game—Jennifer's sudden exit from the barn, Luther chasing them. Clara had dropped her hand and run the other way. Chances were she was well hidden with her eyes closed when her father overpowered Jennifer and threw her down the shaft. It was likely she didn't even see it happen. Jen prayed that were true. And Grunwald surely would dispose of Muncie's body while Clara was asleep, as well as Muncie's truck and Applejack.

Applejack! She'd forgotten about her horse. What had Grunwald done with Applejack? He'd have to get him out of sight. Was he hidden in the barn? Did he cut him loose on the prairie? Surely, he wouldn't hurt him. Or would he? A swell of anger flooded through Jen's heart. Again she tightened her fists and shrieked out in fear and rage and desperation.

But screaming was useless. She knew it was. The crumbling walls of the gloomy shaft seemed to fold in, obliterating every sound. Still she gulped the air and tried, until exhausted, to vent her anguish and frustration with a wild cry. Finally she gripped a clump of weeds and bowed her head, easing the rhythm of her breathing to a normal pace. If she was going to survive, she needed to stay in control.

But no sooner was that determination made than she found herself jerking in horror against a fresh enemy. Something was crawling along her arm, some desert insect creeping through the tumbleweeds. She brushed the creature away, never seeing it in the darkness. This wouldn't be the last of these cave dwellers. Her eyes began to brim again with tears. There were spiders, snakes, and lizards in these pits, and in that respect, she was not alone. Remaining frozen for several moments, she anticipated being bitten or crawled on again, and when that didn't happen immediately, she sighed gratefully.

A shifting of the planks above startled her and set her heart racing. The crease of light widened to a triangle, and Luther Grunwald's shadow filled it. Jennifer lay still as the man peered down toward her in the darkness, moving from side to side for a better angle. Not certain how much he could see, she tightened up. Only her eyes moved with him in the light. Every ounce of strength she had was spent on trying not to breathe.

"You alive down there, girl?" yelled Grunwald. "I'm still thinkin' that you are."

He must have backed away from the pit then, for the triangle grew brighter for a moment. Then Jen heard shuffling, and the shadow loomed again. "No one's gonna be lookin' for you here," cried Grunwald. "I got rid of your horse, and I got rid of Muncie. There's no reason for anybody to come around."

Jen took a few quick breaths as Grunwald backed away again, this time kicking one of the planks over on its side. Finally, she gave up trying to remain rigid, for her body was trembling and there was nothing she could do to stop it.

Cold tears came with the pumping of her heart. What the man above her would do next, she couldn't tell, but she'd lost all hope that there was any goodness in him.

Then a stinging pebble came, a small rock Grunwald tossed downward into the pit. The first one cracked against the sand above Jennifer's head and landed in the tumbleweeds. But the second hit her shoulder and the third her cheek, bringing a soft squeal of fright that she could not hold back. Finally she screamed, flailing her arms against a barrage of little stones the man began to pelt at her from the mouth of the shaft, chortling as he did so like a schoolboy bully with a caged animal to tease.

"Haw! I figured the stones would rouse you!" He laughed. "I figured you wasn't dead. At least not yet."

"Stop it! Stop it!" Jennifer wailed, as the last of the rocks flew down. "Why are you doing this to me? You need to get me out of here!"

Grunwald dropped to his knees at the mouth of the pit and squinted at her. "Hey, now," he croaked, "you yell like that again, I'll bring boulders next time 'stead of pebbles. You got that? Why, it wouldn't take nuthin' for me to dump a big ol' heavy rock down there that would crush you like a walnut, and don't you forget it. I didn't ask you to come nosin' around my place. I didn't mean for things to happen like they did. But you seen what you seen, and I'm not goin' to jail for it." Grunwald lowered himself to his belly over the sandy mouth of the shaft and looked stealthily from side to side before he spoke again. His pale thin hair was hanging around his ears. "You yell like that when anyone's around, I'll put a bullet in the fellow on the spot, and that's a promise. You hear me, girl? Yessiree, you better keep nice and quiet, and pray that no one catches an idea that yer there. The sheriff, that bishop daddy of yours, that deputy kid that was with 'em the other day, or anybody. They come snooping 'round here askin' questions, you better hope they don't hear nuthin' from this pit. I don't want to shoot nobody else, but I will if I haf to. I got nuthin' to lose now." He paused. She could hear his smirk when he added, "I could send a bullet in your direction, too, just as easy as I did those rocks. You keep that in mind the next time you think about opening your mouth to holler."

The man rose up on his haunches, still pondering the darkness of the hole. "Hey, you hear me, girl?" When Jen remained silent, he finally stood straight up, paused to brush the gravel from his shirt, and then began to replace the planks. "You hurt?" he asked. "You bleeding down there?" The triangle of light began to close. A shower of sand had covered Jennifer, but she still blinked at the sun in its tiny crease. Grunwald's voice was hollow through the wooden cover. "Like I said, I didn't ask for this to happen," he called, "and there's nuthin' I can do about it now. You best go to sleep and hope it all ends quick. It's a shame, but that's the way life goes sometimes, even for nice young gals like you."

Chapter Eight

As a second night fell in the valley with no sign of Jennifer Brodie, authorities began to turn their attention to previously convicted felons or sex offenders in the area. Sheriff Castle hated to broach the subject with the bishop, but the possibility that the girl had simply fallen from her horse and was lying injured somewhere was fading with every passing hour. With little local help, he'd called neighboring agencies in almost immediately—Utah and Salt Lake Counties were both helping out, as well as deputies from Grantsville and Magna. Since, in the words of Sheriff Castle, Dillon Dancie had turned to Jell-o on the case, so upset you'd think the devil had spooked him, Mike Castle officially had taken the young man out of the field. Instead, Dill was to run down every person in the county who'd had a scrape with law enforcement in the past five years, particularly those crimes involving violence against women.

The kid had spent most of his time pacing the floor and wiping tears away, and no one blamed him. He could hardly contain himself, Castle noticed, even in front of a computer screen. Countless times Dill kicked the wastebasket, angry at being tied to a desk while everyone else was out searching for Jennifer. And when he did begin to focus, he found no promising leads. Tooele County had its share of domestic violence cases, custody battles, and assaults, but most of the men could be readily accounted for. Some were currently in prison. Others had left the area. Those few who remained were tracked down and easily cleared.

On Wednesday, Dill went to see Rex Brodie. They sat in the bishop's home office, both in pain but the older man better suited for his burdens.

"I'm going to pieces over this," said Dill. "I can't stand the thought of Jennifer . . . golly, Bishop Brodie, we've just got to find her! She's everything to me! Everything! We can't just sit here! We've got to find her! She's got to be okay!"

Dill sobbed like a child, and Jennifer's father held him in his arms and let him cry. "We're going to find her, Dill." He tried not to let Dill feel how much his own hands were trembling as he patted his shoulders and gripped his arm.

Rex knew something of his daughter's romantic ambivalence over Dillon Dancie. They had always been close, Jennifer and the bishop. "I want to marry a man who really, really loves *me*, Dad," she'd told him once, "not just as a friend or as a great date or as a good Mormon girl he has a lot in common with, but someone who loves me with all his heart and soul. Someone who'd be sad—no, heartbroken— if I was no longer in his life for some reason. Maybe that's selfish, but that's how I feel."

"I think everyone yearns for that kind of love, sweetheart," Rex had told his daughter.

"How can you ever be sure you have it?" asked Jen. "How will you ever really know?"

"You'll know," he'd replied.

Brodie remembered that conversation now as he watched Dill Dancie walk wearily to his car. The boy hadn't eaten. He hadn't slept. He could barely stand up straight. Evelyn and the bishop were as physically and emotionally exhausted as Dillon was, but they were family. Maybe Dill loved Jen with more than surface intensions as well. Brodie wept after the young man had gone. He was almost overcome with grief. If this crisis was proving something about Dill's capacity for love, he prayed his daughter would live to someday realize its depth.

* * *

"It's as if the girl just vanished into thin air," said an exasperated Sheriff Castle to his clerk on Wednesday afternoon, "and I know *that* didn't happen!"

He fell into the chair behind his desk and was running his fingers wearily through his gray hair after a sleepless night, when the clerk, Kate Renstrom, responded to his lament by offering him the phone. "It's Salt Lake County," she said. "Their helicopter may have spotted something." Len Gardner was out on patrol, so besides Kate, the front office was empty.

"What you boys got?" Castle barked into the receiver, grunting an "uh huh" at the answer, and then, "I'll meet you there in half an hour."

Castle looked up from the phone to see Dillon Dancie standing at his door and hoped the kid hadn't heard Kate's words about the helicopter. He wasn't ready to spend time calming Dillon down again—didn't have time for it—so he mumbled passively, "Got anything?"

"No, not really," answered Dill, but he approached the desk with a sheet of paper and laid it in front of Castle. "This is that record on Bill Muncie from when he was picked up the other day with stolen tags." Castle noticed Dillon's hands were trembling.

"So? What about it?"

"Nothing, I guess."

"Well, if you see a connection here, just say so." Castle was growing impatient. "What's Muncie got to do with this, Dill?"

Dill was nervous, proving what Castle still believed. He wasn't up to the challenges of this particular case. He was too personally involved. "We were just out there at his place," he said, "checking on this charge against Muncie, and Jen was with us. Remember? It just seems like they're tied in somehow. I saw this pop up on the screen, and that day came to mind. That's all." He straightened up and wiped his eyes with his sleeve and worked to get control of himself. "Maybe old Bill Muncie is a worse fellow than everybody around here thought."

Castle stood up and shuffled around his desk, suddenly feeling sorry for Dill. He put his hand on his young deputy's shoulder and tried to calm him down. But Dill's notion about Bill Muncie being somehow involved with Jennifer's disappearance carried no weight just then.

It wasn't until he'd driven thirty miles into the western desert, following the coordinates Salt Lake County had given him, that he came upon a scene that changed the entire case and turned his thinking upside down. In an isolated patch of scrawny cedar trees and sagebrush, the helicopter and its crew and a shiny green GMC pickup loomed before him. The chopper had spotted the truck earlier that morning. Inside the cab was the body of Bill Muncie, a pistol near his hand and a bullet in his heart, and even more disturbing clues were yet to be discovered. Mike Castle suddenly had a whole new mystery to consider, and Jennifer Brodie was as much a part of it as the drifting sand that swirled around the scene.

* * *

News that a body had been found in the desert traveled quickly through the little towns of Cedar Fort and Erda and into the outskirts of Tooele. The friends and neighbors and ward members who had been diligently searching for Jennifer Brodie felt a jolt of agony at the first whisper, believing it must be the sunny-haired girl. Sheriff Castle hurried to the Brodie place as fast as he could to set the record straight— although his news was not all good.

He sat in the comfortable living room as Bishop Brodie paced the floor, Tony fidgeted nearby, and Evelyn, looking like a ghost, trembled on the edge of her chair. Her eyes were ringed and swollen. She had aged ten years in two days, Castle thought, as he stared at her and cursed his mission. Several relatives had arrived to offer their support—Evelyn's sister from Salt Lake, Rex's brother and his wife from Milford. The brother was staying in a motor home in the yard. Friends and ward members came and went.

Castle wanted only the immediate family around just now, and that's how it was. "I know you've been hearing things," he began, "but don't believe them. We *did* find a body this morning about thirty miles to the west out by Miller's Crossing. It was Bill Muncie, and it looked like he'd killed himself."

"Bill Muncie?" Rex Brodie was incredulous.

"He was in his green truck and had a pistol in his hand. 'Course we're checking everything out. But suicide is what it looks like. Shot through the heart."

Tony looked wide-eyed at his father. Evelyn was still shivering in her chair, pale and thunderstruck.

"So this has nothing to do with Jennifer?" asked Bishop Brodie.

Castle hesitated. "Well, we don't think so . . . we hope not."

"What do you mean, you hope not?" Brodie was suddenly alert.

"Well, Rex, it is somewhat of a coincidence that you and I *and* Jennifer were just out there at Muncie's place the other day talking to Grunwald. I mean, it does cause you to wonder about things," Castle said uncomfortably.

"What kind of things?"

"I don't know. It's just an odd coincidence, that's all."

Bishop Brodie was more upset than Castle had ever seen him. "You know something you're not telling us, Mike?"

"No, I don't. That's the awful part of it. And I'm sorry as I can be about all of this. But I'd like a hairbrush or comb of Jennifer's, if you can give me one. It might come in handy later if we need to check some things."

With an audible groan, Evelyn rose suddenly from her chair and left the room without another word. Tony pounded a decorative pillow with his fist before tossing it across the room and stomping out through the kitchen, letting the back door slam behind him.

Rex crossed the room and grabbed Castle by the shoulders, shaking him hard as he looked him squarely in the face. "Jenny's dead, isn't she? You've found her and you're scared to tell us."

"No, as far as I know, that's not true." Castle stiffened.

"Go ahead and tell me, Mike," pleaded Brodie, unbelieving. "I'll break it to my wife." He was quivering now, his jaw set, his brown eyes glaring, and Castle had never seen a man quite so stricken.

"Listen, Rex," he said again, "I'm telling you, I don't know where Jen is. I'm going to do my best to find her. I promise you." He wasn't sure if Brodie could even hear him, and the man's grip was like a vise on his shoulders. The pressure only eased when he heard Evelyn's voice behind them and turned to see her standing in the archway of the living room holding a hairbrush and a comb.

"These are Jen's," Evelyn rasped. "If they can help you find her, of course we'll give them to you, and anything else you need."

She departed quickly, and Rex Brodie accompanied Castle to his car, apologizing for his loss of temper. It was then the sheriff told Jen's father what he didn't want Evelyn to know just yet. "Rex, we found long blonde strands of hair in Bill Muncie's truck. There's no reason to believe they're Jennifer's, but we're going to have them tested against what's here in Jenny's brush. It'll take a little time."

Brodie was anxious again. "What's Muncie's situation? I know he was divorced. Did he have a girlfriend, a daughter?"

"His ex-wife, Maxine, is a brunette," said Castle. "There's no daughter, and I don't know of any girlfriends lately, but it's early in the investigation." He got in the car. From the front seat, he looked up at Brodie sympathetically before he turned to drive away. "Try not to worry," he told the bishop, knowing the task was beyond any father's capacity.

After turning the hairbrush and comb over to county forensics, Castle made his way back to the office, mulling his next move. He'd already spoken to Maxine Davis, the victim's ex-wife. Maxine had remarried a few years before and now lived happily in Erda. She was sorry about Bill but knew nothing regarding his recent activities and hadn't seen him in more than a year.

Clyde, Bill's brother, was claiming the body when the medical examiner was finished with it. He seemed appropriately distraught over his brother's apparent suicide, shaking his head and saying he couldn't figure it out. "Bill had no worries that I know of," Clyde said. "He got taken to the cleaners when his marriage ended, but time passes. Bill's moved on. No, I just can't figure this. As far as I know, he had plenty of money and not a care in the world."

"Any trouble with women?" Castle asked, thinking of the long, blonde hair in the truck.

"Oh, heck no," said Clyde. "Bill swore off women after Maxine left him. I don't think he's had so much as a date since then, and that was six or seven years ago."

"You're sure he had money? Bill didn't have collection agencies breathin' down his neck?"

Again Clyde shook his head. "The folks set us up pretty well in property, and Bill's rented out most of his share. He doesn't have to work, but he always has his hand in something. He invests in this or that and has always made it pay. No, Bill's never needed money. He's got plenty. He'd rather keep it than spend it. That's been his problem. Probably what cost him his marriage once upon a time."

Castle listed all these things in his mental reference book, thinking of the green GMC where Muncie spent the last minutes of his life, thinking of the stolen license plates he'd filched from Grunwald's shabby wrecking yard when he could have purchased any car he wanted. He wondered what made some men so tightfisted while others were such wanton spendthrifts. Both types were foolish as far as he was concerned. Most of all he wondered whether Muncie's miserly habits had become lethal in some way. He also had to wonder about the shot. Suicides generally aimed their pistols at the temple or through the mouth, very seldom at the heart.

At the office, where Castle stopped to pick up some papers, Kate had unsettling news. "Dill Dancie bolted out of here ten minutes ago," she reported. "I would have called you, but it only just dawned on me that he's probably headed to Luther Grunwald's."

"What makes you think so?"

"He's been pacing around here like a plucked chicken ever since the word came in that it was Bill Muncie's body in that truck. He seems to think there's a connection between Muncie and his girlfriend, and Grunwald's place is the only thing they had in common."

"That's a stretch," said Castle. "The kid's grasping at straws. It's crazy. We have no reason to think the girl ever laid eyes on Bill Muncie just because she happened to visit a piece of property he owned. He needs to stay here or at home and leave the investigating to me, instead of stirring up trouble at Grunwald's."

Kate shrugged, lifting both hands to show Castle what she was up against. "The kid's wild in love, Mike," she said sadly, "and I'm afraid this isn't gonna end well for him, whether Grunwald's involved or not."

Castle thought of the long, blonde strand of hair in Bill Muncie's truck and guessed Kate was more right than she knew. "I'd better get out there before we have another problem on our hands."

Chapter Nine

DILL DANCIE BOUNCED HIS CAR up the back road to the Grunwald place in a billow of heat and dust. Rolling to a stop in front of the cluttered yard reminded him of the week before when Jennifer and Bishop Brodie were there, and he clenched his fists and closed his eyes, squeezing away the tears that suddenly brimmed as that image came back to him. Jen had been gone over two days, more than forty-eight hours. And yet only a while ago, she was right here, happy and beautiful and trying to help a little girl.

Dill looked around for Clara but didn't see her. The ragged front porch of the trailer was still covered with its awning, which stood askew on frail legs and ominously warned visitors to keep their distance. The yard was anchored by Luther Grunwald's business, a fleet of cars in various stages of life and rehabilitation. Most of them were destined for the scrapheap, Dill observed again. Apparently Grunwald made a living with them. Dill wondered why some folks were content to live the way they did, in the midst of trash and squalor. It was one thing to be poor, he thought, another to be filthy and neglectful. And to expose a child to the ugliness. That was the worst of it.

Grunwald came out of the barn just then. He was as slanted and grubby as the barn itself, Dill thought, and both had their share of secrets.

"What d' ya want?" called Grunwald. "Aren't you that deputy kid that was here with the sheriff the other day?"

"Yeah, I am," spit Dill, marching toward him, "and now I'm back!"

"Well, what are ya here for?"

"I'm here to have a look inside your barn and in that mine shaft too! The one you were supposed to put a fence around." Dill motioned with his shoulder toward the direction of the pit near the brush and boulders some twenty-five yards distant.

"You got a search warrant?" demanded Grunwald.

Furious, Dill pushed past the man. "Get out of my way!"

Grunwald was right behind him as he trudged toward the shaft. "I don't know what ya expect to find in that hole," he said. "I've thrown a few weeds in there, some trash. It's a devil of a long ways down, and you don't even have a light."

"Just stay out of my way," Dill hissed back. He had reached the mouth of the shaft and had begun lifting and kicking aside the lumber Grunwald had placed there. When the opening was large enough, he dropped to his knees to look inside, squinting and wiping the dust out of his eyes.

"Black as a tomb down there," remarked Grunwald, standing above him.

"Shut up, Luther!" snapped Dill.

Grunwald chuckled. "Shoulda brought a flashlight, son." The man raised his voice as if he were proud of his words and wanted the neighbors a mile away to hear them. "You even shoulda brought some help. Comin' out alone like this isn't gonna get you anywhere, even if you did find anything."

Dill lay flat out on his stomach and peered as far as he could into the bowels of the pit. All he could see in the darkness was a trace of some kind of branches or brush, probably tumbleweeds. "Jen!" he yelled. "Jennifer! Can you hear me, Jen? Are you down there, babe? It's Dill. Call up to me if you can! Jennifer, are you there?"

For a long time Dill listened hopefully. The sun was warm as he lay there in the sand. The cloudless heaven above him was never more blue and beautiful. But the dark hole offered nothing but cold silence. He got to his feet a much older man.

"What made ya think the girl was anywhere around here anyway?" Grunwald stood behind him. "I never saw her before until last week when she and her pa came snooping around here botherin' Clara. If you can't keep track of your girlfriend, that's your problem. I don't know why you think she'd be anywhere near here."

Grunwald's smirk was all Dill could take, and he pushed the man and then attacked him with his fists. "You know something you're not sayin'," Dill yelled as Grunwald tried to fend him off, holding up his arms and hands, blocking every blow. "Where is she, Luther? Where's Jennifer? You tell me where she is, or so help me, I'll—" They were still near the mouth of the pit and about to slide closer as they tussled, but suddenly Dill felt someone grab him from behind and heard Sheriff Castle talking in his ear.

"Come on, boy, ease off now," said Castle. "That's it; slow down."

"Your kid there's got a hair-trigger temper," said Grunwald, backing away and brushing himself off. "You better keep him corralled a little better."

Feeling the fight fade out of Dill, Castle pushed him aside and faced Luther. "The guy's girlfriend's missin' two days now. He's not himself; that's all."

"No call for him to come around here makin' accusations," snorted Grunwald. He watched grimly as Castle shoved Dill back toward the yard. The young man went reluctantly, glaring over his shoulder as he walked. Grunwald moved ahead of the sheriff, letting Castle follow him.

"Bill Muncie's dead, Luther. You hear about that?"

"Muncie?" Grunwald stopped in his tracks, and when he turned to face the sheriff, his expression had changed. "What happened to him?"

"Found him in his truck this morning out in the west desert. He was shot. Could be a suicide, but we're not sure yet. That was why Dill made some connection between this place and his girlfriend's disappearance, in case he didn't explain himself. The timing is coincidental."

"I don't see how either one of 'em has anything to do with me," said Grunwald obstinately.

"When was the last time you saw him, Luther? Muncie, that is?"

"Oh tarnation! Let me think. It's been awhile. A couple of weeks maybe. He comes by to collect the rent on the fifteenth. Never misses rent day, you can bet. That's probably when it was, though I couldn't swear to it. He's in and out sometimes, if he needs spare parts. A real miser though. Won't give nuthin' for what he takes from me. Not even a little off the rent." Grunwald suddenly caught himself. He eyed the sheriff and hesitated. "I guess I shouldn't speak poorly of the dead. You say Bill shot himself?"

"Looks that way."

"Well, I can't say I'm surprised. Ol' Muncie didn't have a friend in the world that I knew of. He was so tightfisted with his money, a millionaire, I hear, but as greedy as a banker in a gold mine. Like I say, no friends. No enemies either. So I guess suicide's your answer."

"What about women?" asked Castle carefully.

This got a slight rise out of Grunwald. His gray eyes narrowed. "That's Muncie's business. I wouldn't know about that."

Castle looked over at Dill, who seemed to have forgotten about Luther. The young man was gazing dolefully toward the old mine shaft, the shaft which had yielded nothing in his desperate search for Jennifer. He was ashen-faced. Feeling Castle's eyes on him, Dill turned and walked up to Grunwald with his hand extended. "I'd like to apologize, sir. I had no right to come on to your place like I did and make accusations and search the pit without a warrant, and I especially had no right to push you around. I hope you'll give me a break here and try to understand the circumstances." With that, he swung on his heels, and the two men watched him march toward his car, get in under the wheel, shut the door, and drive away.

"Dumb kid," muttered Grunwald, as Dill's Chevy left the yard.

"I'm still worried about that mine shaft, Luther," said Castle, disgusted with the man and hoping to subtly suggest that the county had some leverage here. "I've submitted an order for a shovel and a dump truck to get the darn thing filled. You know how requisitions go. It takes a little time. But I reckon a fellow will be around sometime next week. We'll let you know. In the meantime, I'm glad you got those planks over it. I wouldn't want that girl of yours to fall into the thing." Castle looked around the yard, trying to end on a friendly note. "Where is the girl, anyway? I usually see her around when I come by."

"Clara?" Grunwald motioned toward the trailer. "She's inside." At that moment, the little scarecrow emerged as if on cue and hid behind the porch post, peering out at the sheriff.

"Howdy, Clara." The lawman waved. "You like being out of school?"

Castle expected no response and got none. He left a grandfatherly smile and turned toward his Jeep. It didn't seem like a good time to ask Grunwald about Muncie's stolen license plate again. Like the mine shaft, it was completely irrelevant to the case, and Dillon Dancie had just made a fool of himself finding that out.

Chapter Ten

MERE YARDS FROM WHERE THE sheriff pulled his Jeep onto the dirt road, Jennifer Brodie lay curled up in the tumbleweeds, still shivering. The terror would not fade. The thought of Dill standing over that open pit, unaware of the danger at his back, left her numb and panic stricken. She let long seconds pass before she allowed herself to breathe. She waited even longer before she felt safe enough to move. Even then, she could not hold back the tears.

Hearing Dill call out her name, she had recoiled in utter anguish, yearning with every fiber of her soul to answer him. "Here I am! Oh, Dill, you've found me! Get me out! Please!" She had even seen Dill's face, just barely. He was far away, and she had purposely sunk down in the branches of the tumbleweeds, covering herself, so he wouldn't see her. But she recognized him, his square jaw and high cheekbones, his curly, close-cropped hair. Oh, how wonderful and alive he looked! It had taken all the self-control she had not to cry out but to remain frozen and perfectly still, terrified of Grunwald's threat. *"I'll kill whoever comes around. He hears ya scream, I'll put a bullet in 'im. You just remember that!"*

Jennifer remembered, and every second Dill stood above the shaft, she died a little. But she'd stayed hidden, wrapped up in the darkness, submerged among the weeds. In his impulsive eagerness, Dill had brought no flashlight, no rope, no weapon.

When the voices faded, Jen was aware of some sort of scuffle above her and the arrival of Sheriff Castle. She heard heated words but couldn't tell exactly what they said. She thought of screaming then, while there were two men there to help her, *before they walked away.* Maybe Grunwald would be caught off guard. He wouldn't have time to pull his gun on anybody. She almost gave in to the terrible urge to save herself. She took the risk, but when she opened her mouth to cry out, no sound came.

She gulped the air and tried again, and this time a small croak was all that she could muster. "Dill?" she managed, but the word was hardly above a whisper. Another attempt produced a thicker groan. "Help me!" But there was little energy behind the effort. She was still paralyzed by what Grunwald might do, and she'd been more than two days without water. Her mouth was sandpaper dry, and soon she knew that any words were simply powder on her tongue and useless.

Soon she thought she heard an engine start and another engine fade, and then the shaft grew quiet once again. Had she lost her chance at rescue? Was life and breath right there at her fingertips and she'd let it go? Would it ever come again? Maybe Grunwald had been bluffing with his threat. His shooting of Bill Muncie had seemed an act of impulse and not cold-blooded murder. Would Grunwald have really shot Dill and Sheriff Castle just for hearing her screams? She considered the question grimly. He'd thrown her in this pit, perhaps on an impulse, but he'd done nothing to get her out.

Apparently he intended to let her die, and that was murder, pure and simple.

* * *

After Dillon was gone and the terrible burden of panic had lifted, Jennifer felt herself sliding into a quiet delirium. It had been nearly three days. She was cold, thirsty, and now weak from having no food. Her wounds burned, her stomach growled. She was grimy and filthy, and with no alternative, locked in the arms of the tumbleweeds as she was, she had wet herself. It dawned on her, as she pondered Grunwald's threats, that she would die in this place, in this narrow pit of rock and sand, that no one would ever find her, that this would be her grave.

For a time, the faces of her parents floated before her in the darkness, but she couldn't bear their grief, especially that of her mother who was so tenderhearted, so she forced herself to think of Dill. And not in a sad way. She would fend off her woes by thinking of him in an earthy, attractive, romantic way, as if she wasn't in this hole. She mused for a moment, trying to stir herself completely out of her misery long enough to concentrate on real life and Dill. Golly, he was hot! He was one gorgeous guy! Still he *was* rather reserved with people, not overly social the way she liked to be. They had dated since junior high and had gone out fairly steadily for two years, but she didn't know if she really loved him, and she certainly didn't know if he loved her—at least not until today.

He'd never said too much about it. Everything was fun and games up until now. Of course, Dill knew his mission was coming up, and maybe that had kept him from making any serious declarations. Even now, she wasn't sure if it was

Dillon Dancie she was meant to marry. It was fun to cuddle in the front porch swing with him after a late date, and their summer romance was going to be all a girl could dream about before his mission and her return to Provo split them up again.

Sometimes she told herself he was a shallow kid, maybe even a little beneath a college girl like her. Then she'd kick herself for her elitist attitude. Dill Dancie and his kind were the salt of the earth, and she knew it. The truth was, she concluded, she might not be good enough for *him*. Still, could she really love him? And was his love that deep for her? She didn't know yet about herself, but the ache she'd heard in Dillon's voice as he called her name at the mouth of the sandy shaft told her there was more to his anguish than what just any good man feels for some lost victim. She remembered telling her dad once that she wanted to be loved deeply by the man she married—very, very deeply. She hadn't been sure that Dill was capable of that kind of love. Or at least she hadn't felt it from him at that point. Now there was that ache in his voice. It was something she had never heard before.

The reverie did not last long. Soon the delirium took over. Her body began to tremble. The pounding of her heart grew louder in her ears. Why was she even thinking of a future with Dill Dancie or anybody else? She was sinking. This is where it all would end. She closed her eyes, too weak to fight the darkness anymore.

Luther Grunwald came again that night when the yard and the trees and the trailer were cast in shadow, and little Clara was probably asleep. It was a cloudy time when a storm was about to burst forth in a thunderous rumble. But while the rain delayed, Grunwald took advantage. He moved most of the planks away and sat at the edge of the pit, taunting Jennifer with his sour whine.

"Hey, wake up down there!" he called, tossing a handful of sand and pebbles over the side. "You did a devil of a job today, keepin' quiet. I'll have to give ya that."

When Jennifer didn't answer, he threw more sand and stones, and when this drew only silence from the shaft, he got up and shuffled off until he found a rock a little smaller than a bowling ball. This he aimed at the center of the pit and sent it down with some thrust behind it. It grazed Jennifer's cheek, missing her head by quarter of an inch. She cried out as it stung her shoulder.

"Ah, I knew that would get a rise outta you. You weren't asleep!" Grunwald cackled. "You were just tryin' to fool ol' Luther." He sat down again on the planks and put a grass stem in his mouth to chew, as if he wished to begin a pleasant conversation. "That deputy kid sure put up a fuss over findin' you," he mused. "He's sure darn lucky he didn't, or I woulda had to shoot 'im. I'da done it too. I had my pistol in my pocket, and I was ready to make my move if he'd a caught on that you was down there. You done good, girl. That fella musta meant a lot to you, for you to keep all quiet the way you did. I suppose it wasn't easy, but ya done it good."

Grunwald was silent for a moment. Then he seemed to change position and slide along the planks. Jennifer could barely trace his shadow in the starlight in the tiny opening above. "I thought about killing that boy anyway," he said suddenly. "The kid was getting awful close to findin' you, and I thought about lettin' him have it then and there. It woulda been easy, too, behind him like I was. But I'd made a bargain with ya. If you'd stay quiet, I'd spare whoever came around, and I keep my bargains. I can't say the same for that backstabber Bill Muncie! No, he was never one to keep a promise. The old penny-pincher!"

Jennifer swallowed hard and listened as the man slid along the planks again. His words were becoming slurred as if he had been drinking. A new fear flooded through her. "You want to know who's really to blame for all of this?" continued Grunwald. "That no-good cheapskate Muncie, that's who. We had a deal, an honest shake-hands money-making arrangement, and the scoundrel broke his word. Yeah, I shot him! I'd worked hard for what he owed me, and there he stood in my barn, tellin' me he wasn't gonna pay. Well, you shoulda seen his eyes pop when my gun come out!"

Her heart pumping, Jennifer wanted to scream. What kind of business? Why would Bill Muncie owe his renter money? Why would anyone kill a man over a stupid business deal?

"But I didn't start out planning to even fire the gun," said Grunwald, softening a little. "I was so mad it just happened." He paused, and when he spoke again, it was with added strength. "But now that it's done, I'd do it again. I've got nuthin' to lose. One killin' or two? It don't matter anymore. You remember that, girl, if somebody comes nosin' around again. I'm resigned to it. Nuthin' bothers me anymore. I'd drop the hammer in a second. You bet I would. So why haven't I? I don't know. I reckon I'm lettin' *you* stay alive right now just for the fun of it. It's kinda nice knowin' where you are when nobody else does and teasin' ya a bit about it. I got one up on ever'body that way! And I got someone to taunt and talk to in the dark of night, for a while anyway, until the fun wears off. Heaven knows, weird little Clara ain't no good at conversation!"

Grunwald stood up and stretched. Was he about to leave? Jennifer sensed as much, and she heard the man's tone change. "So like I say, you can blame Bill for your troubles.

And that brings to mind another thing I'm beginnin' to savor about these circumstances. Someday soon the law will be countin' you against Bill Muncie too. It come as an added bonus I hadn't figured on at first. Why, the way I've got things fixed, they'll think Muncie killed *you*, and no one will ever know the difference. Good ol' Bill Muncie." Grunwald chuckled. "I'm gettin' him back double for cheatin' me!"

Just when Jennifer thought that he was gone, Grunwald stuck his head down into the pit as far as he could drop it. "And just in case you're wonderin' about that bug-eyed little girl in the trailer sayin' anything to anybody, Clara doesn't talk, ya know. She doesn't talk, and she doesn't write. And no one would believe her if she did. She's 'impaired,' as they say politely. She don't know what's going on. And what's more," he added, laughing, "the little beggar isn't even mine!"

* * *

It rained on Wednesday night. There were warning signs in the afternoon as gray clouds boiled up in the west and the air grew heavy. Finally, just at twilight, a sky-splitting torrent washed down out of the hills, soaking every piece of the county in its path. The water flooded the low-lying places, leaving puddles and even pools where the slightest dips or larger holes had been. Canals and ditches were filled, outdoor troughs amply supplied. Thirsty gardens gladly took their share. On the desert, the water ran in rivulets to nourish Hawthorn bushes, the Utah juniper, and the other flora of the vast wasteland. Cottonwood leaves fluttered against the force of the raindrops. Blooming flowers—the cliffrose and wild rose and sego lily—bowed their heads, waiting out the storm.

At the Grunwald place, the rain drummed and splattered noisily against the metal roof of Luther's trailer and against the steel of his rusty cars. His chickens huddled in the barn. The debris floated to new places of display across his yard. In her bed, little Clara shielded herself against the lightning and the pinging raindrops with her pillow, hiding under it and wishing day would come. Grunwald sat up late in the main room of the trailer, wondering about the girl at the bottom of the mine shaft. "She's gonna get wet tonight," he chortled to himself. His eyes narrowed as he thought of the fight she'd put up against him and how she was apparently still surviving after all these hours and days. *Maybe it wasn't the best thing to do, throwing that girl in the pit like I did. It was like killin' Muncie though. It was a spur-of-the-moment thing. I had no choice at the time.*

Grunwald settled back in his chair and rubbed his whiskered jaw. His pale eyes began to water. "I shoulda killed that girl right off," he murmured to himself, "and not let her suffer so." He listened to the rain a moment and straightened out his tired legs. "Yeah, that woulda been the kinder thing to do. Nice and quick, like Muncie. As it is, she'll suffer. The water'll seep in that pit, and she'll be a drowned rat in the morning, all wet and cold. Yeah, I shoulda done the kinder thing. I guess I still can, if she lasts much longer."

* * *

A few miles away, Rex and Evelyn Brodie also listened to the thunder and the rain. Evelyn was quiet, afraid to speak, but Rex knew what she was thinking. She trembled as he held her close, and he could almost feel the pounding of her heart. *Wherever she is, I hope she's warm and dry. Please protect her from the storm. Please guard her, until we come . . .*

Chapter Eleven

AN OLD MAN RUMBLED INTO Grunwald's yard on Thursday morning. Jacob Archer was known about town as a castaway, one of those ancient veterans of several generations back who seemed to linger in the present long after he'd become irrelevant. He lived at the county nursing home but still drove his own car and made a habit of cruising the outlying roads of Tooele, "checking on the parameters," he liked to say. He was a long-time widower with hair as white and tossled as cotton in a windstorm and chin whiskers just as pale. No one paid him much attention except to say, "Howdy, Jake," or "How's it goin', Arch?" and sometimes notice how his eyes had a glaring quality when they focused hard at anything he found of interest.

Luther Grunwald knew Jake Archer. The grizzled fellow liked to talk about old cars, and Luther had a lot of them. Archer spent an occasional afternoon hobbling among the decrepit metal skeletons on Grunwald's place, tinkering with this twisted door frame and that rusty drive shaft. "A regular graveyard here," he'd say to Luther. "Bones of many a fine automobile, tales of many a wild Saturday night."

"I suppose," Grunwald would return laconically. He put up with Archer but didn't particularly like him. He never purchased anything and was probably prone to steal a hubcap or hood ornament, if he could get away with it. Luther always had to keep an eye out, and this annoyed him. He was particularly nervous on Friday morning, since the old man seemed less interested in the cars for once and more focused on something he'd never asked about before.

"I had a dream last night, Grunwald," Archer said the moment he got out of his car. "I saw that old pit of yours, the one just under that boulder pile, there across your property line." Archer raised his arm and pointed toward the shaft, twenty yards away. "I saw it plain as I'm seein' it right now. When I woke up this morning, I knew just where to come."

"You crazy old coot," laughed Grunwald. "What are ya talkin' about?"

"I'm talkin' about my dream, the one I had last night. I seen yer pit there, plain as day."

Grunwald turned his back, giving the man no interest. "So you saw the pit. So what?"

Archer followed him as he walked, still pleading his cause. "Dreams mean things, Luther. They really do. 'Specially ones as clear as that one was."

Grunwald faced Archer and threw up his hands. "Like I said, you saw the pit. So what?"

"Ain't you been reading the papers or listening to the news?" pressed Archer, his brow dissolving into wrinkles. "The valley's got a girl missing, a bishop's daughter. She was out riding three or four days ago and never made it back. The horse came home without her. Ya musta heard about it. It's set up a scramble in this place not seen in twenty years."

"Yeah, I heard about it," said Grunwald, disinterested.

"Everybody and his brother is looking for the girl," said Archer, sticking close to Grunwald as he moved along. "Some think she's dead by now. Others figure she up and ran away. Most don't know what to think or what to do, now that everywhere's been searched."

Grunwald shot Archer a sullen smile. "Maybe they should offer a reward," he said off-handedly. "Sometimes money works when nothing else will get ya what ya want."

"I wish they would," said Archer furtively. "A reward would be right nice."

Struck by the old man's tone, Grunwald stopped and listened. "What were ya tellin' me about that dream ya had?"

Archer suddenly leaned forward and got close to Luther's face as if sharing a long-kept secret. "Well, I think I know where that gal is."

"You don't say." Grunwald's eyes narrowed.

"I think the gal is in that pit of yours," said Archer excitedly, his eyes ablaze. "I seen it in my dream."

"Did ya now?" said Luther, smiling.

Jake Archer nodded foolishly. His eyes drifted in the direction of the mine shaft, its opening concealed by the wet planks, still dripping after last night's rain. "It was clear as day in my dream," he repeated. "The missing girl is in that shaft, and I think we oughta take a look."

Grunwald paused, frowning and considering. Archer's eyes were round and wide. He looked as eager as a small boy in a candy store.

"What makes ya think the girl's in that shaft of *mine*?" asked Grunwald, raising a malicious eyebrow. "The thing's all boarded over. How would she have gotten in there?"

"Danged if I know," the old man fired back. "Maybe she was curious and just fell in. I don't have all the answers. But like I told ya, it was in my dream. I saw it clear as day."

Grunwald relaxed, dismissing Archer as the crank everyone always thought he was. He shrugged and walked away. "Well, I'm not goin' to let ya go diggin' around in that shaft 'cause ya had a dream. Not when there's no reward for it."

Archer stood and stared longingly at the shaft. "You ain't even gonna let me take a peek?"

Grunwald had picked up a wrench from a tool chest near the porch and turned to face Archer. "Go ahead if ya want to. Have a look."

Jake Archer hesitated and then shuffled slowly in the direction of the pit. Grunwald followed a few yards behind. At the trailer door, little Clara slid from the other side of the screen and sat down on the porch to watch.

"I think you've just got caught up in all the excitement, Jake," taunted Grunwald, as he followed Archer. "This missin' girl is all anyone is talkin' about, and I think it's got stuck in yer mind."

"I seen her in this shaft, plain as day!" cried the old man without stopping.

"It'll be a lot of work to scour that deep of a hole," insisted Grunwald. "You got a light, Jake, or a rope? What about a ladder? I sure wouldn't be going to all that work and trouble without being paid for it. There's got to be some kind of reward on the other end, Jake. You should clear that up with the authorities before you even start."

They had reached the edge of the pit as Grunwald spoke, and Archer was looking dubiously at the planks, which lay wet across the mouth. "How long you had this boarded up?" he asked.

"Oh, a week or so," Grunwald answered. He watched as Archer made an effort to push one plank aside with his muddy boot and then bend on his knee to peer into the pit.

"Hello in there!" The old voice cracked as it bellowed into darkness of the hole. "You in there, girl?"

The shout was met with only silence.

Archer tried again, bowing his head as low as he could go and still maintain his balance, moving the plank as far as it would go without Grunwald's help. But there was no answer when he called the second time. Nor the third. And he could see nothing in the dark eye of the shaft. His vision had deteriorated through the years, and only in his dreams were images very clear.

Grunwald was there to pull old Archer to his feet when he finally gave up. "Like I told you," he said, "I'd make sure there was a reward posted before I'd worry about this, Jake. That gal who's missin', you see if her daddy has any money and what he's offerin'. I'd do that before I'd go crawlin' around in the sand because of some dream I had."

Archer mumbled to himself as Grunwald led him stumbling back to the yard. "I thought for sure she'd be there," he muttered.

"Yer used to seein' that old shaft when you come to look at my cars," Grunwald reasoned. "Folks has been fascinated with it over the years. Bill Muncie told me that."

"You reckon that's why I dreamed of it and put it together with the missin' girl?"

"Could be," said Grunwald. He had Archer back to his car and into the driver's seat, and he gave the old man one last piece of advice before he sent him on his way. "Don't say nuthin' about the girl being in the shaft to no one else, Jake. Don't say a word. Not unless a reward is posted and you see it in writing. Then it might be worth a chance. Otherwise, you'll just seem like a fool. Most folks don't believe in dreams, Jake." Grunwald put a friendly hand on Archer's shoulder to make his point. "I let ya take a look, and nuthin'

was in the shaft that ya could see or hear. There's no reason
to go no further and come out smellin' foolish, unless there's
money to be made. Until there is, I'm tellin' ya not to say a
word about yer dream, and I won't either. Why, Jake, even
if there was some reward bein' offered, I might think twice
before I told yer story. That gal ain't in that pit out yonder,
and I'd be rippin' a good friend and a good mine shaft over
nuthin'!"

"Yer right a course," agreed Archer wearily, still eyeing
the pit with disappointment as he turned the key to start
his car. "I ain't gonna say nuthin' more. It was just a dream
I had."

* * *

Sheriff Castle was worried about the long, blonde strand of
hair they'd found in Muncie's truck. He dreaded seeing the
look in Bishop Brodie's eyes if it proved to match the samples
from Jennifer's brush. Knowing your missing daughter had
been anywhere near a dead man before she disappeared
would be more than most folks could handle. And Brodie
would have to tell his wife, which would be another soul-
wrenching challenge altogether. While he waited for the lab
results, Castle tried to focus on what he already knew instead
of what probably lay ahead. It wasn't much, but it kept him
from going crazy along with everybody else.

Castle wasn't ready to call Bill Muncie's death a suicide.
This business about the stolen license plate still stuck in his
craw. The medical examiner's report was inconclusive. The
bullet that killed Muncie came from the gun in the seat
beside him under his hand. He could have shot himself, or
it could have been a set-up. Only Muncie's prints were on
the pistol. But that arrest in Wendover. That kept gnawing

at Mike. On Thursday morning he decided to drive over and see for himself what the UHP thing was all about.

He met the UHP trooper at a truck stop outside of Grantsville. The man's name was Mark O'Donnell, and he'd already ordered a burger as he greeted Castle warmly. "How's your missing person case going over there?" he asked. "You fellas got your hands full with that one."

"Yeah," said Castle, taking a seat and passing on the coffee. "The girl's a bishop's daughter and as nice as they come. Big extended family. It's gonna be a real shame for a lot of folks if this one turns out bad."

O'Donnell nodded. "I've been following the reports, and of course we been keeping an eye out on this end. You got anything at all to go on?"

"We're waiting on a couple of evidence tests, but there's not much."

The trooper looked at the sheriff, hoping to get their business over before his lunch arrived. "You had some questions about some arrest I made?"

"Yeah, a fellow named Muncie from up our way. You stopped him outside of Wendover a couple of weeks ago, driving a '99 ugly-brown Plymouth with stolen plates. Do you remember that?"

"Sure I do," said O'Donnell. "It was me and Jerry Best. We were riding double that day and picked this Muncie up rattling down I-80 in this junker. I remember him 'cause he was a smirky sort. I wouldn't have stopped him, but the plate didn't look right. It was bent and dirty, and there was something odd about it, like it had been screwed on in a hurry. The guy was nervous, too, once we had him on the shoulder. He kept saying things like, 'You got a drug dog in Wendover?' and 'I'll bet you're wonderin' why a well-dressed guy like me would be driving a piece of garbage car like this.' Anyway, when I ran his plate, you shoulda seen his mouth drop when it came up stolen. He turned humble right away and gave us some cock-and-bull story about borrowing the Plymouth, saying he got it at a junkyard from a friend."

"You believed him?"

O'Donnell shrugged. His burger had arrived, and he was ready to dig in. "Turns out, the tag was stolen, but not the car. The plate belonged to a 1979 Chevy, which was reported stolen a month after it hit the streets and probably chopped into pieces a month after that. It was as old as Methuselah's ghost. So I wrote this Muncie up for expired tags, gave him a temporary, and told him to hit the road. I didn't like the guy. Like I said, he seemed a little anxious but too stupid to cause anyone much trouble. I thought about calling out the drug dog, but he really didn't fit the profile, so I didn't take the time."

"You never saw him again?" asked Castle.

"No, never did. You lookin' at him for somethin'? If you chase him this way, let us know. I wouldn't mind another crack at the snooty slicker."

"Too late for that," said Castle, rising from his chair and reaching to shake the trooper's hand. He thanked O'Donnell and left, still wondering why Bill Muncie was driving a Plymouth with stolen tags outside of Wendover and what it had to do with Jenny Brodie.

There were posters with Jennifer's picture on every tree and pole from Tooele to Cedar Fort by then. So many casseroles and buckets of chicken and hot rolls had been brought to the Brodie house that Evelyn's sister, who'd come from Salt Lake to help, had to stack the excess in the cooling pantry and give some away to the neighbors. Volunteers from every stake in the valley had combed the area on foot and horseback. Men on ATVs had run up and down each known trail and paused at every abandoned hole or cave. Most of these were shallow, offering little mystery. The deeper ones had been plugged up long before, purposely shuttered with fences, wooden planks, and warning signs. Tunnels were always tempting to explore. Castle could remember often letting his flashlight lead him as a boy, taking him farther into the darkness than he ever should have gone, farther than he'd ever let his own son go today if he caught him at it. The deeper desert shafts were generally off limits without proper gear and supervision, but Castle imagined some of Bishop Brodie's friends were taking a few risks on their own as they searched for Jennifer. So far they'd found nothing.

A stake fast was announced for the coming Sunday. Castle, though a member of the Church, was not as steady in his faithfulness as Bishop Brodie. "If the girl's not found alive by Sunday," he whispered to himself, "fasting isn't gonna do a lot of good."

Then Salt Lake called with the lab results, and the sheriff knew that all the prayers and fasting in the world would probably never be enough.

"It's a match," he told Kate Renstrom when he got off the phone. "It was Jenny Brodie's hair in Muncie's truck."

"Oh my gosh!" Kate was shattered. "I can't believe it!"

Castle turned to look across the room to the enclosure where Dill sat hunched at his computer. He'd refrained from scolding the kid for the incident at Grunwald's, realizing just what was at stake and how emotionally involved Dill really was. "I guess I'd better tell him," he said, nodding in the boy's direction, "before he hears it from someone else." He looked at Kate and saw the anguish in her eyes. "Then I better get over to the Brodie place," he added. "It's gonna be a long night there."

When he and Dill arrived at Brodie's and shared what they knew about the match, Evelyn at first refused to listen. Her hands flew to her mouth as Castle carefully explained what the details probably meant. She groaned, hiding her face against her husband and then crying out for Castle to stop. She didn't want to hear another word. Besides, how did they know the hair belonged to Jen? And if it did, what of it? Muncie could have offered her a ride. There were a dozen innocent reasons she might have been in his truck at one time or another. Muncie may be dead, but that didn't prove a thing about Jen's disappearance!

"It's nothing!" she cried. "Nothing!"

Castle stood mute as Rex Brodie tried to calm his wife, and he watched awkwardly and sadly as Evelyn ended up sobbing in her husband's arms.

They sat around the kitchen table then, the five of them—Jen's parents and Tony, Dill Dancie, and the sheriff. Evelyn's sister hustled around, dabbing tears from her eyes and trying to make herself useful by keeping their glasses filled. The stake Relief Society president, Annabelle Tucker, was there and had been since morning. Bob Hanneman, the Church's regional representative for the area, was also in the room just then. Other local leaders had been in and out for the past three days. The Brodies held tightly to each other. Dillon looked wounded. Tony bit his lip and tightened his fists beneath the table.

Castle knew he was the only one who could function at the moment, so he tried his best. "Seems like Bill Muncie might not have been the upstanding citizen we thought we knew," he began, clearing his throat.

"This is all news to me." Rex shook his head. "Muncie's been around most of my life. He's about my age. I don't know him well, but I never thought of him as anything but a regular guy. I mean, his family has a name in this valley."

"You know about those stolen tags the UHP nabbed him for," said Castle. "I talked to the officer who picked him up, and he claims Bill was acting really strange for a guy who owns a chunk of Tooele County."

"What do you mean, strange?" said Hanneman.

"I don't know. They wondered what a well-dressed guy like Muncie was doin' in a beat-up old Plymouth, for one thing. He was nervous too. He seemed worried about a drug dog searching the car. At least he mentioned it."

"Did they search him?" Brodie wondered.

"No. Once they ran the tags, they let him go."

"Where's the car now?"

"It's back at Grunwald's. Remember, we saw it the other day when we were there, the '99 Plymouth. Kinda beige. Ugly brown, the officer called it."

"I remember," Brodie said.

"I still don't see what this has to do with Jenny," cried Evelyn, her eyes red and a tissue shredding in her hand. "This hair you claim is hers was found in Muncie's truck not some old Plymouth! Why aren't you focusing on that?"

"They're just trying to track Muncie's recent movements, Evelyn," said Rex gently, "trying to figure the man out."

Castle watched as Evelyn glanced away, ready to collapse into tears again. He could see Rex trembling as he held her arm as if her terrible anguish surged through him, equaling his own. Castle knew it wouldn't be long before Rex turned to the only thing he knew. "I think we need a very powerful prayer right now," he said, mustering all his authority as a bishop and all the emotion he felt as a father. "I think those of us in this circle, in this room, and at this table, those of us

who knew Jen best or who were a presence in her life, need
to join together here and now and pray to God that we can
find her."

Without another word, those who were sitting at the table
knelt down by their chairs. Those who had been standing
dropped in between them, joining the circle, grasping hands
in fellowship and love. They bowed their heads in humble
solicitation and called upon the Lord with full and heavy
hearts for His tender mercy. Ward members, friends, family,
and community volunteers had prayed for Jennifer during
the past three days, but this petition was unique. Mike
Castle—more earthly lawman than orthodox believer—had
never had a spiritual experience quite like this.

"Our Father in Heaven," began Rex Brodie. The robust
tones of righteous authority that only the faithful possess
were punctuated by the broken voice of a stricken man. He
said many powerful things in the unforgettable prayer, but
the theme was potent: "We, a handful of Thy children, have
joined together with grieving hearts on behalf of a beloved
daughter who is lost from us, and we plead with Thee, dear
Father, guide our search, tell us how to find our girl . . . and
protect her till we come."

When everyone was up again and quietly embracing and
shaking hands, Brodie declared directly to Sheriff Castle,
"Mike, I want you to take me to where you found Muncie
and his truck."

"It's about thirty miles out," said Castle. "Muncie and
the truck aren't there anymore, of course, but the spot's been
flagged. We can find it."

"That's where we need to start," said Brodie firmly. "First
light, we'll head out there with enough gear to stay awhile if
we have to."

Evelyn looked up wearily at her husband. "What are you thinking, Rex?"

"I'm thinking about Jenny's hair in Muncie's truck. It's the last proof we have of her being anywhere, so that's the place we're gonna start tomorrow, out there on that desert. Somehow for some reason, Jen was in that truck. Maybe Apple left her afoot and Muncie came along and picked her up. Maybe there was some kind of trouble." Rex glanced at Evelyn, knowing he was in dark territory. "The point is Jen wasn't with Muncie when he died, so that means he stopped and left her somewhere first. I'm gonna find out where, if I have to work forever following tire tracks all over Tooele County."

"I'm with you, Bishop," said Mike. "We'll take off in the morning, and Dill and Tony here can come along to help us cover ground." It was a good idea Brodie had. Castle wondered if it had come as a direct answer to his prayer. He also wondered if Muncie's tire tracks would be long gone by now, erased by the dust and wind and rainstorm of an unforgiving prairie.

Chapter Twelve

IN THE COLD, BLIND DEPTHS of the Grunwald shaft, Jennifer spent the rainy Wednesday night drifting in and out of consciousness. All day—her third now in the hole—her terrible thirst edged her closer to unconsciousness. Her tongue felt swollen in her mouth; her lips were parched and filthy, their corners filled with sand. When the rain came, leaking down between the planks like an errant fountain, she managed to hold her tongue out and catch a bit of moisture dropping down. It was dirty and gritty and more of it splashed in her hair and eyes than hit her tongue, but it was wet and moist and somehow satisfying.

After the storm had passed, water continued to leak into the shaft for hours, turning most of the weeds and trash to mud and slime and bringing sand and dirt down the walls in grimy rivulets. Jenny had never felt so dirty in her life. She was literally an animal living in a hole and no longer a human being with golden hair and brown eyes and a good-looking boyfriend and parents who loved her.

The hunger pangs that had gnawed by the second day had turned to something different now. She hadn't eaten anything since Monday morning, and very little then. She was weak and faint from the lack of food; although, the thought of eating sickened her. She'd grown ill in the darkness of the pit. Coughs and sputters made breathing difficult and labored. When she moved, her shoulder throbbed. When she wept, the tears burned the lacerations on her chin and cheeks. Occasionally, she found herself calling for her mother or for Dill. Once, in a sudden surge of panic, she managed to gather enough air and energy to scream, "Daddy!" But the sound was weak at most, and soon the moment faded into exhaustion.

Worse almost than all of this was the anticipation of Grunwald's taunting. He usually appeared at night, when the beam of his flashlight could drill into the pit, find its mark, and tease her with its glare. He'd come early in the morning, too, before the sun was up, and say things that would turn her stomach. He'd often chuckle that she was still alive. "I can hurry things along in that regard. A boulder or a bullet, take your pick. No need for ya to suffer any more than ya have to." When she didn't answer, he'd merely shrug and excuse his actions. "Like I been tellin' ya, this whole thing just happened. It ain't my fault."

Friday morning, Jennifer was almost too dazed and sick to care. Almost. When she heard the planks begin to slowly slide at the mouth of the shaft, her heart throbbed again with fear. Grunwald's threats were real and her instinct for survival strong. Sand and gravel rained down on top of her as it always did whenever the man came. She blinked at the falling debris, fending off what she could with her arm. She'd hear Grunwald's voice next or perhaps see his light or his gun. Maybe this time he'd carry out his promise and actually shoot at her and "end her misery," as he liked to say. Or maybe he would just talk, rattling on about the injustices of the world and of Bill Muncie in particular. He liked to do that, and he certainly had a captive audience.

Several seconds passed, and when Grunwald did not appear, Jen's fear eased a little. Her heartbeat ceased its pounding, and she strained to listen for any sound. She heard nothing and grew nervous once again. "Is anybody there?" she rasped, as loudly as she could. There was still no answer from above, which led Jen to worry that Grunwald had gone to gather rocks. Her heart began to throb again.

Suddenly a crunching startled her. The frame of sky above her hardly changed, but Grunwald—or something— was definitely there. She braced herself against the expected flurry of gravel or stones or violent curses, but instead, over the edge of the shaft came a small face that took her breath away. It was Clara, as shock-haired and strange as Jennifer remembered, peering down at her with those wide eyes and that odd expression of silent wonder and concern.

"Clara!" Jennifer tried to call but found that she could barely whisper. "Clara, can you see me?" She made an effort to put more energy in her voice, all the while watching the child, who seemed to be aware of her, but, of course, could say nothing. "Clara!" she tried again. "Can you hear me? Nod your head if you can hear or see me. Please, sweetheart, try to let me know."

Clara kept staring downward but did not respond.

"Is your father nearby?" asked Jen hoarsely. "Are you alone?"

Again, the little girl remained still except for her eyes, which began roving about the vertical walls of the shaft as far as the outside light would allow her curiosity to go. Little Clara didn't block the sun at the shaft's mouth as her father did, and when she lay flat, both she and Jenny could catch its reflection. Jen tried to put herself at the best advantage, desperate for some reaction. "Is your father in his truck?" she asked. "Has he gone to town? Has anyone come by?"

Clara looked and listened without a word. Her strange little face never changed expression. She seemed to be watching Jen through artificial eyes. Jennifer coughed and gasped between the questions, and sometimes she had trouble making herself heard above a whisper. But Clara didn't show any sign of understanding. Jen had to remind herself that this girl was only six years old and handicapped. There was very little she could do. Still, when after half an hour she suddenly disappeared, Jenny felt her loss. "Clara!" she called. "Come back, Clara! Don't leave me!"

Once the child was gone, Jennifer wondered if it had really happened. Had little Clara really come? Or was the sight at the edge of the pit only a vision in her mind? Did she yearn so badly for a connection to the outside world that even a helpless waif became a lifeline in her dreams? She waited, listening for any sound. Though little Clara hadn't said a word, Jennifer yearned for her to come again, and with all her heart she prayed for that to happen. Clara! Clara! Jennifer had been so cold, and seeing Clara's face had buoyed her up, had warmed her. She prayed now that such a warmth would come again, and as she prayed, it happened. A warm peace settled down upon her, and somehow she knew that Clara *would* appear once more.

In another hour Clara came, this time barely showing her head over the lip of the shaft. But down through the shadows a capped plastic bottle filled with cold water tumbled well within Jen's reach, the first real drink she'd had in almost four full days. Jennifer shuddered. With trembling fingers she unscrewed the lid and pressed the bottle to her mouth, letting the precious liquid run over her parched lips and into her throat too quickly. She sputtered and coughed and then found herself taking another eager gulp before settling for the more restrained sipping that she knew must follow.

Oh, this was water! This was life! The sand and grit in her mouth were washed away. Her swollen tongue became less painful, her throat less constricted. Grateful beyond words, she consumed only a little more than half the bottle, carefully replaced its cap, and clutched it to her chest as if it alone stood between death and survival, which, of course, it did.

"Thank you! Thank you, Clara!" she called up to the opening of the shaft, hoping with all her heart that the little girl could hear her. But there was no more sign of the curious eyes in the sunlight there. Clara Grunwald had disappeared again.

Able to swallow, able to breathe, able to quench her raging thirst at last, Jennifer was still weak and wretched once she was alone, and sleep came easily. She found herself dreaming of a Primary class and a question put to eight little six-year-olds about a boy named Joseph dropped into a pit by his selfish brothers. Her own words echoed in her ears. *At least some of the brothers probably felt sorry for Joseph while he was in the pit. What do you think they could have done to help him?*

"Water," one little boy had said softly. "They should bring him water," and another added, "Food."

* * *

It was probably just past noon when Jennifer woke again with a start. A high sun was burning directly through the top of the shaft, warming and lighting it a bit and revealing a deep blue sky. Some shuffling above frightened her, and she worked too quickly to make sure the water bottle was hidden from Grunwald's sight. But it wasn't Luther's face that appeared over the rim of the plank. It was Clara again, staring out of the sunshine. This time she pushed a small package over the edge and pinched her brows together as she watched it fall. Jennifer had to wrestle the tumbleweed branches for it, a peanut butter sandwich on stale whole wheat wrapped in a plastic grocery bag. Then came a box of soda crackers, opened but folded shut again.

"Clara! Clara! Clara! Thank you!" she cried as she tore open the bag, suddenly remembering how much she yearned for food. She forced herself to chew more slowly after quickly devouring the first bite. Never was peanut butter such a feast! This time, Clara watched her eat, only scrambling away once the sandwich was mostly gone and Jennifer had thanked her more times than she could count.

A new rush of emotion filled Jen's tired soul. She thought back on the Primary lesson again and suddenly knew she'd soon have a "cover" and a pillow if little Clara could possibly arrange it. True enough, before evening, a lumpy pillow came bouncing down the shaft, together with a small, moth-eaten quilt that smelled like a campfire. Jen would have been astonished, except for the power of faith that she'd been raised to count on in a time of crisis. And if there was any doubt at all that little Clara was remembering what Jennifer had taught, all wondering ceased late that night when the child made her last visit to the hole and dropped something down that was in some ways more precious than the water and the sandwich. Clara was holding a flashlight this time, and Jen was partially blinded by the beam as the little girl tossed an item over the edge and let it fall. It landed in Jen's hands—the threadbare rag doll that Clara had always clung to like a comfort blanket, its button eye missing and its yarn hair looped and tossed.

Everyone had fallen silent and turned together to one end of the semicircle, where little Clara Grunwald was holding out her doll.

"That's silly," giggled the Bradshaw boy. "Joseph wouldn't want a doll!" The children laughed, fidgeting on their chairs and dubiously eyeing Clara's proffered doll.

Jennifer was quick to rescue her. "Oh, I think that's a great idea, Clara. Our toys can often be a comfort to us when we're lost or lonely. I know if I were in a pit, I'd want my favorite doll with me!"

Clinging to the doll there in the darkness, Jennifer began to weep and then to sob. As well as thanking Clara, she thanked God, too, thanked Him with every ounce of strength she had for preserving her thus far and for sending an unlikely little angel to virtually save her life.

* * *

Her stomach jerked and rolled as she regurgitated some of the bread and peanut butter in the night. As hungry as she was, she had swallowed too much too soon for her empty stomach to not rebel. Later, when the nausea faded, she felt stronger. The water helped as well. Not only did it quench her thirst, it cleansed her—a little moisture here and there on her grimy, tear-stained face. And even that lifted her spirits and dulled the sour smell that had sickened her. When sleep finally came, a little hope came with it. For the first time in five nights, she didn't shiver against the chill of darkness or droop her head into a patch of sticker bushes. Clara's old quilt warmed her. The lumpy pillow provided a soft place for her head. Never was she more grateful for small gifts. Her sore shoulder still throbbed, but the quilt and the pillow offered some comfort even here.

Grunwald appeared the next morning. In her childish efforts to push the planks back into place, Clara had left the mouth of the pit open more than normal, and Luther's shadow blocked the early rays of sunlight seeping through the widened crease. He paid little attention to the difference, shoving the boards aside without a pause. Apparently he'd been absent all day Friday, and now he was curious. "You still breathin' down there, girl?" he called. "Are you still hangin' on? Send a little holler up to good ol' Luther, darlin', so I know if you're still among the livin'."

When there was no sound from Jennifer, he paused, and she could see him bend to squint harder into the darkness. "I'll have to throw another rock at you to wake you up, if you don't answer me!" he hissed. "It won't hurt ya if yer dead. It might smart a little if yer not!"

Jennifer tried to remain silent. The food and water had emboldened her against his threats, but she was still sick and nauseated and finally couldn't keep from coughing.

"Haw! There ya are!" said Grunwald. "I figured you was still down there." He took his familiar perch on the edge of the hole, his legs dangling down into the darkness. "I've been gone, ya know. I took a little drive up to Tooele all day yesterday just to see the lay of things. I hung around the coffee shops and the car repair places. A fellow can learn a lot just by doin' that, ya know." Grunwald pulled up his leg and laughed. "I don't suppose I missed much here while I was gone." Then he looked over his shoulder, probably eyeing the shabby trailer where he lived. "Clara didn't bother you, did she? I usually lock her in the house when I leave for very long. This time, I forgot." He paused and chuckled again, delighted with his observation. "It's a funny thing about Clara though. She don't care about nuthin' but herself and that raggedy doll she carries around. There's a good chance she don't even know yer here."

He pitched a few pebbles into the shaft, and they fell harmlessly into the tumbleweeds. "Like I told ya, Clara don't really belong to me, ya know. No, a dumb mute like that didn't spring from my loins, and that's a fact. She's her mother's child. I come along after she was born, and her daddy had run off and left 'em both starvin' up there in Brigham City. Clara musta been no more than two years old. I took 'em on 'cause Clara's mama was a real looker. She made me adopt the girl, wanted everything nice and legal. When she died in that car wreck, I hung on to Clara for the money that the accident insurance brought me, though I never had no fatherly feelings for her, weird little urchin that she is."

Jennifer listened to Grunwald's selfish whine and wondered what he would do to Clara if he knew the little girl had brought her food and water. She prayed for Clara now, as well as for herself. A grimy angel needed tender mercy, too, and Jen was compassionate enough to see that in some ways the child was in a more vulnerable position than anyone else.

Chapter Thirteen

WEST OF THE GHOST TOWN of Bauer, where the dry sand was still cold in the pale morning sun, Mike Castle and Rex Brodie stood beside the county Jeep surveying the distant hills. Castle had risen before dawn, stirring up a flame in the coals they'd left smoldering in a fire pit the night before. He'd wrapped a biscuit with bacon in tinfoil for each of them—Tony, Dillon, and the bishop—and the food was hot by now. The sheriff himself might have been tempted by a sizzling cup of coffee, but he was well aware of the company he kept, and he remembered the power of the bishop's prayer. He was a believer in the faith of his forebears whether or not he always strictly followed the Church's teachings. Working with the underbelly of society had given him a skepticism about life, to be sure, and now Rex Brodie was an impressive puzzle to him. He wondered how a man could even function under the circumstances, and here he was, strong and determined and willing to go to any length he thought was halfway viable. That is, if he thought he was being "guided by the Spirit."

Castle's question had rumbled through his head all night. If a higher power was so much involved, why wasn't the "spirit" around to protect Jenny in the first place? Where was her guardian angel when whatever happened to her happened? Why did the "spirit" always come along with guidance after the fact? The truth was after so many days, they were liable to find Jenny's body out here on this desert before they ever found the living, breathing girl herself. There was some good in "spiritual guidance," he guessed, but he would have appreciated the "blessing" coming a bit earlier, before there was only a body to retrieve and so much sorrow on account of it.

He'd broached the subject with the bishop in a simple way, not really saying all that he was thinking. Castle had watched Brodie walk behind the Jeep and kneel down for a personal communion with God while Dill and Tony were still asleep. Now, as Dill was washing up some distance away and Tony was just stirring in his sleeping bag, he thought of what Rex had said when he returned from praying and he'd put the question to him. "Why would the Lord let this happen, do you think? If prayers can save Jen now, why didn't they protect her last Monday when she went out riding?"

"I don't claim to have all the answers, Mike," said the bishop wearily. His eyes were bloodshot and sad. "I think it has to do with moral agency. God doesn't generally step in and stop evil people from doing bad things. Evil is part of this mortal world, and it always will be. We can and should do our best to protect ourselves, but it touches all of us at one time or another—some worse than others. But that's how we learn and gain experience, vicariously or otherwise. I suppose it's how we learn Christlike compassion, by feeling real sorrow. I don't know all the answers, but something tells me I'm better off staying grounded in that faith."

"Why even pray, then, if God just lets bad things happen so you can suffer?" At that moment, Castle could hardly bear to look at Bishop Brodie, so kind and stalwart in his character. He was the last man on earth to deserve this current pain.

"God doesn't change what bad people do, but He does help good people deal with the adversity. He keeps them strong, soothes the wounds, blesses them in countless ways, shows them how to learn from the experience. The closer we remain to Him, the more evident these blessings are when trials come. I believe that, Mike. I've believed it all my adult life. I have to believe it now."

Castle nodded. With all his heart he hoped Rex Brodie's faith would turn out to be more than well-articulated theory.

Brodie seemed anxious to talk practically to Castle before Dill and Tony joined them, and the subject soon turned to their failures of the day before. They had easily found where Muncie's GMC had been. The recovery team had flagged the spot. The place where the helicopter landed was obvious as well. They were even able to differentiate the tire tracks of Muncie's truck from those of official vehicles on the scene, knowing county Jeeps and cruisers as they did. But the tire tracks didn't take them very far. There was no road nearby. The truck had meandered cross country, grinding up the sand and gravel as it careened through sage and brush and gully wash before coming to rest where Muncie fired his last shot. Sometimes the tracks faded in the sand or were lost in patches of weed, and then took up again a few yards farther on. Tony or Dill would shout, "I found 'em!" from up ahead in one direction or another, and the search would continue. Finally, though, no more than half a mile east of the resting spot, the truck tracks disappeared altogether.

Castle and the bishop drove in the Jeep for another mile and searched every inch of sand. Dill and Tony took the

Brodies' Suburban to explore southward, where the ground was level and dry. Dill walked two miles from their starting point, finding nothing. The tire tracks had vanished. The sky was as wide as a blue dome above them. The endless prairie spread out, a blistering vista in front of them, and they had no more clues to follow.

"I'm not giving up, Mike," Rex said decisively. "I know you think we should end things out here because we've lost the tire tracks, but I'm not ready to do that yet."

The four of them stood by their vehicles after breakfast, sipping water, kicking sand, and restlessly discussing their next move.

Dill was angry. He kept pumping a clenched fist into his palm and gritting his teeth. "I'm with you, bishop!" he cried. "I'll stay out here forever, if you say so. You're gonna find out what happened, and I'm gonna be here when ya do!"

"We may be runnin' up a blind alley," suggested Castle carefully. He was reluctant to pull rank on Brodie's prayers, but the trail had gone cold.

That's what Brodie had wanted to speak of privately that morning out of earshot of Dill and Tony. "Stay through this afternoon," he'd pleaded with the sheriff. "If that truck was here and Jenny's hair was in it, well . . . it's something of hers. I just have a feeling about it." Brodie paused, and Castle hated to imagine what the exhausted, anguished man was thinking. A boundless desert lay before them, and the girl had been gone four days. He had prayed so hard, so powerfully.

"I'll stay through this afternoon," said Castle now. "Then I'd best head back. You can keep Dill out here with you. I can maybe find another lead in town."

It was settled then. They determined to search the gullies and washes and tree-lined patches near any clutter of stones or boulders where a body might be hidden, though they didn't speak out loud as to why they made that calculation or why they marched in somber silence through the harsh terrain. They covered many miles, driving across the level places, climbing or searching on foot where they couldn't go by vehicle. More than once Brodie said he probably should have brought his horses, and sore feet made Castle and the others agree. They ate the sandwiches they'd brought along and drank water and soda from the sheriff's cooler, but they found nothing, no sign that told them they were even close.

Tony, frustrated, tired, and with a teenager's impatience, finally threw up his hands and dropped down in the sand. Tears came to his eyes, for Jenny and for his own lack of stamina. "She's not out here, Dad!" he cried. "We've been chasin' our tails for two days now, and she's just not here!" Hanging his head so no one would see his face, he ran his fingers through his hair and tried to get control. "We could search out here all summer long and never find a thing. Don't you see, Dad? She just isn't here!"

Rex Brodie dropped to his knees beside his son and put his arm across the boy's shoulder. Dill and Castle looked away to save Tony a bit of shame, but they listened to the bishop's words and were heartened by them. "Somewhere, wherever she is, Jen knows we're giving all we have to find her. She can feel how hard we're trying. If she's still alive, that may be why. But even if she isn't, somewhere her spirit knows we're here. I want that, Tony. Whatever happens, I want Jennifer to know how much she was loved and that we did everything we could to bring her home."

* * *

Mike Castle returned to Tooele late that afternoon. He decided to see if his time could be put to better use looking further into Bill Muncie. Average guys usually didn't suddenly become violent toward women overnight. That still bothered Castle, as well as Muncie's strange run-in with the UHP. There were several things which needed a closer look. He had come to believe frankly that Jen Brodie was dead, and after hearing the bishop's sad speech to his son, he believed Rex Brodie thought so too. There was no man he admired more, and Brodie had the right to keep searching in the west desert as long as he felt the Lord was guiding him, but, as sheriff, Castle needed to look into some other possibilities.

"There's cell coverage if you don't get too far out," he told Brodie as the two shook hands and parted. "I'll keep in touch."

Brodie and the two younger fellows stood watching him, hands on their hips, as he got into his Jeep. They were sunburned and disheveled. "How long you figure to stay out here?" asked Castle as he turned the key.

"Another day or two, I imagine," answered Brodie. "We've got food enough for tomorrow. The ward is fasting Sunday, and so will we. After that, we'll see."

Castle nodded. "Good luck." His tires stirred the sand behind him as he headed to the north. A new idea had struck the sheriff, one he didn't want to share with Brodie until he'd explored things a little more. Bill Muncie was in that old '99 Plymouth just days before he died. He'd driven it to Wendover and maybe even farther, and no one knew why. Muncie had a perfectly good truck. What was he doing in that old Plymouth with a stolen plate? That question had never been answered to Castle's satisfaction. A joy ride? Who goes joyriding in an old clunker? And Muncie got all antsy when UHP stopped him. He seemed to be nervous about something. A drug dog, maybe. Well, that Plymouth was still sitting at Luther Grunwald's place. Castle decided it required a closer look. He would need a search warrant, and that would take some time. But it was something. Sunday loomed. He'd see what Luther had to say before the judge signed off. He put in a call to the office to check with Kate Renstrom and got a funny story.

"Old Jake Archer stopped in here this morning and wanted to know if there was a reward posted for the missing girl." Castle could hear the disgust in her voice. "He swore he knew where the girl was. When I asked him how, he said he saw the place in a dream, as plain as day, and he would swear on the book he was certain of it."

"Well, where is it?" Castle scoffed. "We need all the help we can get."

"Jake wouldn't tell me. No, he said he was no fool. He'd take the reward money first, thank you. I told him we'd let him know the minute we got the final figures put together. Poor old fella. I wish we could count on a few good dreams in this case comin' true."

Chapter Fourteen

IN HER HELLISH, NARROW HOLE, Jennifer spent Saturday worried about Clara. The little girl hadn't reappeared at the opening—forced to stay away once Grunwald was back on the premises, Jen surmised. Clara was smarter than people gave her credit for, but could a six-year-old keep a secret from a desperate killer very long? The question gnawed at Jen, even as the hours passed. She was hungry again. The crackers didn't last. Her stomach growled incessantly, and she needed water. The bottle had been empty a long time. Her throat was parched from coughing and from thirst.

In spite of her misgivings, every sound from the eye of the shaft above brought a surge of hope that it was little Clara bringing another peanut butter sandwich or a bottle of water. But Clara never came, and deep down, Jen was glad. She dreaded what would happen to Clara—to both of them—if Grunwald caught the child supplying her with aid. "She isn't even mine!" Grunwald's evil taunt echoed in her ears. No, she couldn't bear the thought of Clara suffering because of her. She'd rather die here in this hole, she decided, than have that happen.

In the midst of her anxieties, Jen began to count her blessings. The sandwich and crackers had provided nourishment, and the quilt and pillow Clara brought had taken the chill away, allowing her some degree of warmth and rest. The water had literally kept her from drying up and dying. Even Clara's seedy rag doll, which Jen clutched close in the tumbleweeds, gave her a connection with the outside world. Someone above knew where she was and had bestowed upon her a most prized possession to remind her she was not alone.

Suddenly she was frantic to help Clara. Suppose Luther had already discovered what the little girl had done and was brutally punishing her? A new urgency surged through Jenny's soul. She looked hard and long toward the top of the shaft, squinting at the crease of light and its beam that sifted down into the hole. At that moment, she would have traded the world for a rope, a hook, a ladder, a pick, several boxes to climb on, or even strong enough beams of wood to wedge between the walls and lift herself up high enough to scramble out.

But there was no wood. The tumbleweed branches were thin and prickly and mostly rubbish by now anyway. And the distance to the top of the shaft was perhaps sixty feet since the tumbleweeds had lost their "lift" and become mostly a pile of branches and sticks. It was farther than any scramble could take her without good equipment. Still, the prospects energized her and gave her something to think about. She felt along one side of the shaft with her hands and discovered it to be mostly solid rock, not sand and gravel as she expected. She remembered outside, where the shaft began, a pile of boulders marked the farthest edge of the property, and she assumed that this narrow pit butted against the underground remnant of those rocks. Exploring the other three walls inside the shaft, she found two wooden support beams opposite the stone and half buried in the dirt. She could feel them in the darkness with her hands and knew they were wide and substantial, though logic told her that they couldn't have extended very high.

She judged herself to be fairly close to the bottom of the pit. The stack of buoyant tumbleweeds had saved her from greater injury because they were new and tightly positioned. If, in the last few days, they had settled into twigs and refuse, it probably meant that she had sunk deeper as well, although it was hard to know. She'd considered making her way down through the rubbish to the bottom, probably no more than four or five feet below. Perhaps she would find some side tunnel that led to safety. But she knew there was a risk in going lower and ending up worse off than she already was. She hated losing sight of daylight or falling farther from it, even when it was only a glint between the planks. The sun was her lifeline. Nights were terrifying. She couldn't risk slipping too far from the sun.

So her exploration extended upward along the wooden braces and dirt walls of the shaft as far as her arms would reach. Wincing with every motion of her injured shoulder, she persisted against the pain, letting most of the work and weight fall on the other limb. Guessing that the beams led to some kind of starting point or platform below the mouth, she moved her fingers along the edges, searching for some niche to grasp. The sand was hard and mixed with rock and gravel. The walls had not been touched for decades, except by creatures that crawl and bite and sting and glare with beady eyes at those who don't belong.

Working blind, Jennifer kept her fingers moving. She knew her nails were black, her hands chafed and scratched. Sand fell in her eyes and hair whenever she tried to raise her head. A shower of sand dropped down at one point and left her choking and wheezing and spitting grit that crawled along her tongue. She would have cursed if Grandma Bentley hadn't made her promise on her baptismal day, nearly twelve years before, to "never let dirt fall from her own lips, no matter what dirt others might let fall on her." Jen smiled at that maxim now and the irony of it here. She had kept that promise, and she loved Grandma Bentley enough to keep it still, no matter what!

At last she felt an edge that made her fingers pause and then dig all the harder. Halfway between the two brace beams, there seemed to be a horizontal bar of wood, like a ladder rung, embedded in the wall. Fairly deep, with slivers of it piercing her hands as she worked, the step was old and crumbling, but its very existence sent a thrill of hope through Jenny's heart. If this was a ladder rung, there must be another one above it, and another after that. Surely the miners who drilled this shaft so many years ago and braced it with the beams would provide themselves some way in and out. Again she remembered no ladder at the mouth or as far down as anyone could see in the dark. But the beams were holding up these walls, and at some point in time, someone had been serious enough about the shaft to need more than a rope to climb.

She edged around the sides of the rung enough to provide what felt like a solid niche and then pulled herself up and reached to find another like it just above. After a few minutes of searching, there it was. She could feel the second step of the wooden ladder with her fingers. Buried deeper in the wall, it was wedged in so far that a cascade of sand came down before she could actually grip the bar, but she knew what she was touching, and the sand in her eyes only made her laugh. She was used to working blind by now, and she was suddenly eager for what the next upward grasp would bring.

It brought a girlish giggle of joy. Another ladder rung was buried in the wall two feet above the last, and another after that. Jennifer couldn't tell what anchored these hidden wooden steps. They were barely edges now, creases in the sand and dirt. As she ventured upward, trusting each wooden foothold with her weight, she wondered if each bar was part of a chain—not a metal chain, but a series of steps covered by years of dirt and rubble, maybe a real ladder, or what was once a ladder, underneath. Perhaps there was more stone behind the wall of dirt that she could feel, and the build-up of fragile sand could have been more recent. The early miners might have hammered the rungs into the crevices between the rocks, and time itself had hidden them. They seemed stable enough to climb on and certainly worth the risk.

Slowly, she advanced upward, gaining inches as she struggled to find and unearth each roughened stick of ravaged wood, praying each would be in its place like the one before it, hoping each would lead her closer to the crease of light above. The angle of the sun would work against her, but for the moment, that was the least of her fears. Some of the rungs barely jutted from the wall, while others provided a full stepping place once she dug the dirt away. Climbing between them was the hardest part, especially in the dark. She managed to do it by always finding the third rung up and using it for leverage. Still, the process took too long. Soon she looked over her shoulder into the blackness of the pit and was unable to even reach her pillow or the tumbleweed rubbish or even see them in the tiny rays of light the crease dimly provided. She was clinging to the wall in utter darkness and had to depend on just her feet and hands to guide her.

And there was no turning back. She had reached a point of no return where it was more of a risk to fall backward than to maintain a steady climb. Time was crucial. She could still see the crease of light, but it was fading quickly. The mouth of the shaft was closer and wider, but the angle of the sun was changing, and soon she would lose the light.

She expected some sort of wooden deck or platform to appear, for the brace beams had to end somewhere. Suddenly she reached out in the shadows for the next rung, and it wasn't there. Scraping around in the sand and digging with her fingers, she still came up with nothing—no wooden bar, no branch, no niche, just a sandy wall, nothing on which to step.

"No! No, no, no, no!"

Clinging with her one good hand to the rung she still owned, Jen pressed her forehead against the sand and tried to keep her balance. Her left foot was firmly in the niche below, her right poised to climb, and now she had nowhere to go. She made an effort to gain control, to grow calm, to pray. She had come this far. She would not give up. A swell of determination flooded over her. She thought of Dillon, so frustrated and worried and angry as he stood above the pit just days before. She thought of her mother, how she must be grieving, and of her father, the strong and able bishop, who had given so much service to others and needed her strength now. Mostly she thought of little Clara, for it was the child who was in danger should Grunwald realize she'd turned on him. That image was foremost in Jen's mind as she reached again and stretched her fingers farther, desperately hoping to find another rung beneath the sand. Clara! She had to get to Clara! The eye at the top of this horrendous pit would bring her light and air and freedom, and if she could reach it, she might also save a little girl who lived in a black hole of her own.

Finally, she touched it, something protruding from the sand. In a last-gasp effort at reaching as far up as she could possibly stretch without losing her grip, Jen found another ladder rung. Carefully, against the pain of a bruised and twisted shoulder, she dusted the sand away from a long groove along the bottom of the wood, and soon the bar took shape. It was definitely a horizontal step. She could feel its edges. Guessing she had probably missed the rung in between, she focused her efforts on this one. It was high, and gripping it tightly meant dangling her feet above the lower niche. This cheated her of leverage, and she had no way to advance.

Realizing the pit was very narrow at this point, Jen braced her feet against the dirt and her back against the rock wall on the opposite side. In this precarious position, and still gripping the high rung, she tried inching upward in a vertical direction, hoping to feel the next rung before she slipped. Thankfully, the tactic worked. The wooden step was there, not too high and not too deeply embedded, and she caught on to it firmly just as she began to slide. Her feet dangled for a moment until she found the step again and was secure once more.

Frightened by the near miss, she paused a moment to catch her breath and to simply hug the wall until her heart stopped thumping. She pressed her forehead into the sand and wept, letting the fear and frustration of five days melt out of her. Whether tears or perspiration, the moisture on her face turned the dirt to grime, and she risked a free hand to wipe the grit away. Swallowing hard, she realized she was trembling, although her grip was solid and her feet were more securely planted than they'd ever been before.

"Don't lose it here," she whispered to herself. "Don't lose your nerve." She knew her father would have called it gump-tion or courage. Her mother might have referred to it as some type of faith or perseverance. Maybe Tony would say it was just plain guts. Whatever it was called, she clenched her fist and prayed to keep it. It was all she had.

Once calm, she stretched for the ladder rung above, expecting it to be there and relieved to find it was. It was tedious, treacherous work, for she was high enough now to not only worry about falling but about what to do if Luther came by and heard her busily digging and climbing. He had thrown rocks at her before and once threatened to shoot her.

Pushing that prospect from her mind, she continued the struggle. Carving each buried rung out of the sand brought her closer to the mouth of the shaft, even as it remained out of reach. If she got as far as the ladder rungs would take her, somehow she would find a way to make up for the rest.

But for Jennifer, fate had other plans. Or maybe it was the angels who knew that Luther Grunwald was about to march by with his pistol cocked and his patience stretched. Whatever it was, it came all at once, about twenty-five feet from her destination's edge. Before Jen could sense trouble and scramble back down the steps, a groaning lurch began and then a crack or split of something solid that made Jennifer look up, terrified. Suddenly, the creaking wooden rung she was standing on sagged beneath her feet, and two long vertical side beams of an ancient ladder, hidden beneath the dirt for decades and rotting there like a buried corpse, crumbled through the wall. The beams didn't fall diagonally against the opposite side of the shaft, allowing Jen to dangle from the rung, nor did they break in half, leaving something above for her to reach and grab. The ladder disintegrated vertically from top to bottom, like a tower in a firestorm, its tired wood collapsing where it stood before anything could be saved. In a cloud of dust and sand and gravel, Jenny was suddenly plunging helplessly down to the tumbleweeds again, tumbleweeds which were now only matted, prickly rubbish, offering no cushion at all.

Her scream was muffled by the smothering sand as wooden rungs and side beams turned soft as ash and broke into pieces. And like a collapsing tower, the debris followed her in a billowing, smoky clatter back into the darkness at the bottom of the hole.

Chapter Fifteen

SUNDAY MORNING, SHERIFF CASTLE, WITH Deputy Len Gardner in tow, stopped at Luther Grunwald's place again. Grunwald was outside rummaging through some scrap metal and paused to look warily at the Jeep as it approached the yard. Glancing back at Clara, who was dawdling on the front porch of the trailer, he returned to his work, leaving the officers to make their way to him with whatever it was they wanted.

"Morning, Luther," said Castle when he got close enough. "Me and Len here thought we needed to stop by."

"It's a peaceful Sunday morning, Sheriff," sighed Grunwald without looking up. "Is there no rest for the wicked? I figured law-and-order guys like you would be in church."

"Someone has to keep an eye on things," returned Castle laconically.

Grunwald stood up straight and surveyed the scene around him. He waved his arm in an exaggerated way, mocking Castle's words. "Just what is it you're keeping your eye on here? The junk heap or the outhouse?"

"I'd like to take another look at that old Plymouth Muncie was driving when he got flagged at Wendover, the one with the stolen plate."

After a slight hesitation, Grunwald shrugged. "It's still sittin' there, ugly as Clara's dried-up peanut butter if you ask me. You're welcome to it. Haul it outta here anytime ya want. I ain't got a chance in Hades of sellin' it. I'm sure of that."

While Luther talked, the three of them moved toward the row of cars and trucks along one edge of the yard, the remains of half a dozen vehicles, once new and well made. The Plymouth was where Muncie had apparently parked it over three weeks before, and even Castle had a hard time answering Grunwald's question: "This car hasn't moved since Muncie left it here," he said. "What's this old Plymouth have to do with him killin' hisself, like ya told me? I thought he was in his truck when ya found 'im."

"Yeah, he was," said Castle. He was eyeing the Plymouth from end to end while Gardner popped the hood and puttered about underneath it. "You ever see Bill again after he brought this Plymouth back here?"

"Never did, now I think about it," Grunwald answered. "I suppose that brother of his will be 'round to collect the rent, but I ain't seen 'im yet."

"So Muncie left in his truck and that's the end of it?"

"Yeah, like I told you. So what's this Plymouth got to do with anything?" Grunwald was irritated.

"Probably nothing," said Castle. "The timing's odd; that's all. When a fellow like Bill Muncie commits suicide, you look for a reason, anything out of the ordinary. You want to cross all your t's and dot all your i's before you finally close the case. I'm gettin' a search warrant. Then I'm gonna have Gardner here come back this afternoon with a tow truck and haul this Plymouth up to Tooele. We're gonna sweep the thing up there in our garage and see what we can find, just to be sure. Maybe give the drug dog a go at it, too. The UHP people didn't do that, ya know, and maybe they should have."

Grunwald laughed. "That skinflint Bill Muncie selling dope? Now that's a joke! Like I said, go ahead and take the car. Get it off my hands. Seems like yer barkin' up the wrong tree though. I thought you was lookin' for that bishop's daughter. You found her yet? Seems like that would be more important than some old Plymouth Muncie took joy ridin'. 'Course, who am I to know your business?"

Castle took his time and eyeballed the Plymouth as well as he could. On the surface there wasn't much to see.

After popping the hood, peeking in the trunk, and showing Gardner where he could find the keys, Castle retreated toward his Jeep. He eyed poor little Clara Grunwald on the way. He felt sorry for the girl, shabby in her faded cotton dress, which was too small for her. Her hair was uncombed, her face unwashed and frowning. She's the one who needed to be at church that morning and in Primary with the other children, not out here in this heap of a yard. Castle gestured toward the child, telling Gardner, "Wish I could take that one to church with my grandkids today."

"Looks like Grunwald boarded over that old mine pit," observed Gardner, glancing that way as they drove out. "Muncie should have done it long ago, especially with that little girl around."

"The county should have done it," said Castle, "and we will. I've got a shovel ordered. I don't trust Grunwald's work. He doesn't give a hoot about that girl of his, poor little thing. Putting a few planks across that hole is nothing. We'll get a backhoe in there and fill the whole thing up. That's the only way to make sure it's safe. Dang shafts! They're the curse of the county. Them and folks like Luther Grunwald, who don't seem cut out for having kids."

* * *

Later that morning, Luther couldn't resist a visit to the shaft. Sheriff Castle's useless visit had left him feeling powerful and lucky. He usually came to the pit after dark when he could shine a flashlight, or early, while Clara was still asleep. "Hah," he cried triumphantly to Jennifer. "The cops come, and they don't even look here anymore! They want that ugly Plymouth. As if that's gonna tell 'em anything!"

When Jenny didn't answer, he nonchalantly threw a pebble into the pit and then another and a third. His feet were dangling off the plank into the hole, and he was at his leisure. He looked across the yard toward the trailer, surveying the clutter of the space. Clara had disappeared inside, probably to watch cartoons, he guessed. He felt victorious for having fooled the law again and wanted to brag about it, but he also felt lethargic. It was Sunday morning, which meant few customers, if any, and it was already getting hot. Too hot to worry about heaving boulders down the pit. He would just sit back and share his thoughts with his captive listener.

"Let 'em come and take that Plymouth," he mused. "They won't find nuthin'. Too bad, in a way. I spent some quality hours on that car—skill and quality, let me tell ya." Grunwald put a knee up and rested his chin on top of it. His eyes glazed over as he spoke. For a few moments, he forgot he was speaking to a wretched assault victim in the bottom of a pit.

"It was Bill's idea," he said. "He saw how well I worked with auto bodies, and he knew I had the skill. We picked out the Plymouth 'cause of the hollow hubcaps mostly. But then I found more places I could use—the wheel well, the bumper, even up under the engine mount. There's a hundred places on a car that you can hide marijuana and other dope. I fixed up little pockets everywhere and made it so the stuff would stay just right and we could pack enough to make a killin' in one trip."

It didn't seem to bother Grunwald that no response came as he kept on talking. The opening of the shaft was only a window where he'd moved a couple of the planks away. When his eyes passed thoughtlessly over it, he saw only empty gloom. Dust rose up as some rat skittered by. Otherwise, there was only silence.

"It was delicate work," he continued proudly. "I had to fix the pockets so the cargo was dry and safe, away from curious eyes!" He slapped his knee, remembering. "The dogs could probably smell it if they got a sniff. That was Muncie's biggest worry. 'Can't ya make it so the dog can't smell the stuff?' he'd say to me. 'Well, I guess that'll depend on the dog and how good his nose is,' I'd tell 'im, 'or it might depend on your drivin'. Just keep from getting pulled over and acting suspicious and there won't be no dog to worry about.' That's what I told him. But do you think he'd listen? Oh no! And then who got the blame when everything blew up? Well, you can see why all this happened. That's all I've got to say."

But it wasn't all. Grunwald continued to ponder what had occurred as if he were at a Sunday confessional where no absolution was sought. "I don't know why Muncie wanted to run drugs. The greedy fool didn't need the money. I think it was a game with him, just to see if he could get away with it. You know, put one over on the cops. He had time on his hands. His wife had left him. He was mad at the world. Well, it wasn't no game with me. I needed what Bill offered. I put in a lot of work for what he called a guaranteed jackpot.

"Bill had found a guy in Reno who agreed to pay him five grand to take a few pounds of weed to Salt Lake in that old Plymouth. It wasn't much, just a test, kind of like a dry run, to see if all the pockets would hold up. We were excited. It seemed like nothing but easy. Muncie promised me half—$2,500—for my share when the job was done. Everything was going swell, and then the UHP stopped him for that stolen tag outside, and he came all unglued. He made it into Salt Lake, his nerves as frayed as an old switch cord, and bounced back here swearin' he'd never drive that Plymouth anywhere again. Well, I didn't give a dang about that, but I wanted my money! I wanted my $2,500, and by gosh, I was gonna get it!

"'You sent me off with a stolen tag!' Muncie yelled. 'You almost got me arrested! There's no way I'm giving you $2,500, you stupid no account!' Then the greedy fool threw five hundred dollars on the table and told me I was lucky to get that!" Grunwald paused and straightened his shoulders. He looked at the sun with weary, bloodshot eyes. "That's when I pulled my gun and shot him," he said sullenly. "That's when I killed Muncie."

He moved away from the mine shaft then and didn't seem to care about replacing the planks or whether anyone in the pit had heard what he had to say. It was Sunday. It had been six days since he had shot Bill and wrestled with Jennifer above the hole. Surely she was dead by now. He hadn't meant for it to happen, but there was nothing he could do about it now.

He got in his truck and drove to town, leaving Clara in the trailer watching television. Telling his story as he had, venting into the silence of the shaft, had been therapeutic.

It had reminded him again how blameless he was in all that he had done. What he wanted was a drink, but the bars were closed on Sundays, so he found himself driving by one of the local wards instead, the same one he'd taken Clara to a few weeks back. The parking lot was full. The streets around the building were lined with cars on every side. Even yards and driveways had vehicles parked bumper to bumper in and beside them.

Noticing signs on utility poles and street corners about Jennifer, he stopped to ask a fellow standing by one of them what was drawing such a crowd at the church.

"Special fast today," the man nodded, gesturing at the sign with Jen's photo on it. "Poor girl's missing. Nice kid. It's a shame."

"Well known, huh?" said Grunwald.

"Well loved," answered the man, hurrying on his way.

A mischievous grin crossed Grunwald's lips as he watched the man disappear. The triumphant feeling settled in again, like the high he got when he knew he'd put one over on the sheriff. Only this time, he'd fooled the world.

* * *

At the bottom of the shaft, Jennifer whimpered softly in the darkness. Before, the buoyant tumbleweeds had saved her from more serious injury. This time, it was Clara's quilt and pillow and because she had slid mostly flat against the wall and the fall had not been as far. Still, for all of that, she knew she'd been hurt. Perhaps badly. She must have lost consciousness. For a while she couldn't move or was afraid to, and when she tried, there was so much pain in her leg and hip and right arm, she guessed that she was seriously in trouble. She was in a daze. She couldn't think straight. Did she hear voices? Were there people nearby? Where was she anyway? Why was there so much sand around and something wet? Blood? Or was she crying? Were these simply tears? Oh, where was her mother? Momma would know what to do. Momma always did. Why was it so dark? Why did grit get in her mouth and nose every time she tried to breathe? She hated that. Where was that rag doll? *Oh, here it is. It's so cuddly. Grandma Bentley must have made it.*

Finally, Jennifer slept, but when she woke, the pain had not subsided. Outside, it was daytime, sunny and robust, but she couldn't move without great agony. She heard voices far away. Sheriff Castle? She thought she recognized Grunwald's laughter in the distance and the roar of an engine. Later, Grunwald came to the mouth of the shaft. She could hear him talking, but she was too weak to listen or respond.

When Grunwald went away, leaving her alone, Jennifer wondered how soon she would die. A part of her hoped it would be very soon, and she hoped that for her mother's sake there would be a way she could come back in spirit— bring comfort to her parents and let them know it hadn't been so bad. Grandma Bentley's old rag doll had been there when she needed it the most.

Then, just as Jenny was about to fade into oblivion again, the triangle of light increased. She could hear the sound of the planks moving slightly and could see a tiny face appear over the edge. It was Clara, her bulging eyes peering anxiously down into the hole. Jen could just make out the girl's features in the swath of blue above. She imagined the pronounced pinch between the child's brows. Soon a plastic water bottle came swinging down. This time, Clara sent it down on a long string, which she'd tied around its neck.

Jennifer was almost too weak to open it, but after several tries, she managed. The water was a godsend to her parched throat and her wounds. But it took all the strength she had just to take advantage of the help. Soon the bottle lay beside her, nearly empty, its last drops running wasted in the sand.

"Yes, Clara, yes! Thank you! Thank you!" Jennifer did her best to cry out to the little girl, but she couldn't speak above a whisper. "Please, get help! Don't let Luther know. But somehow, please get help. Please protect yourself. Keep safe! But please find help . . . for both of us!"

* * *

Clara waited at the top of the pit for a good half hour, saying nothing, dawdling in the sand, hoping her Primary teacher would speak again. The hole was too dark for her to see much more than shadows, but she knew Jennifer was there. She couldn't hear her as she had before, and she was sad. She waited, knowing Luther would scold her if he returned and found her by the shaft, so she kept an eye out for his truck and was careful not to stay too long. Later she remembered about the peanut butter sandwich she meant to take to the pit with the water bottle. But Luther had come home by then and had eaten it himself.

Chapter Sixteen

"WE'RE NEVER GONNA FIND HER, are we, Dad?"

Tony bent over his meager breakfast Sunday morning—meager because he had no more appetite for dried eggs cooked over a camp stove. "Jen's gone, and all our searching isn't gonna help."

Brodie knew about the special fast, knew the members of the stake were gathering that morning for him and Evelyn and Jennifer with their prayers and their compassion. He told Dill and Tony to go ahead and eat. They couldn't hike these deserts on empty stomachs, but he was trying to keep the fast, for Jennifer and for those who were doing it for him. Dill refused. "I'm not hungry," he whispered. Brodie knew that wasn't true.

Rex Brodie looked down at the boys as they sat hunched around the fire. They were sunburned and dirty, their faces somber, their bodies spent. The three of them had covered a twenty-mile circle of sage and sand and futility on Saturday, and their eyes were dull and lifeless now with no hope left in them. Dill was angry, his youthful passion showing in the way he ground his teeth and bit his lip from time to time.

Tony was more subdued, even fearful. He was still a kid. Nothing like this had ever entered the safety of his family circle before.

"There's a long canyon up ahead," Brodie said in answer to Tony's miserable surrender. "It runs about a mile and cuts fairly deep in spots—lots of brush and scraggly cedar trees among the rocks, as I recall, hard to see what's at the bottom. I'm thinking we ought to check it out. We'll drive along the top and look it over. If there's nothing promising, we'll head for home this afternoon or evening. You guys have done your best out here."

Gathering their gear, packing the Suburban, and moving through the sand again, they seldom spoke. Dill sat in the backseat and stared out the window, the line between his brows furrowing deeper as the hours passed. Bishop Brodie drove, trying to avoid the sharpest bounces since Tony drooped beside him in the passenger seat. They were miniscule under a broad sky, the car a toy on a trail of sand.

"I wish I hadn't been such a jerk sometimes," murmured Tony, "with Jen, I mean." He sat up and snapped his head back to get the loose hair out of his eyes. "I was always saying stupid things."

"You were a little brother," said Brodie gently. "You still are. Little brothers tease and annoy their sisters. That's what they're supposed to do. You're perfect at it."

Tony shrugged miserably. "Most little brothers get a chance to grow up and make amends."

Brodie didn't answer. The long knife of a canyon lay just ahead, and he began to focus on where best to skirt its edge. He remembered tramping this wasteland as a boy, hunting jackrabbits along its bottom. It was steep and narrow and would be difficult to navigate on foot. It was several miles from where Muncie's truck was found and out of their search range, but Brodie felt something drawing him to look in this direction. He said nothing specifically to Tony or Dill and didn't know himself if this was just a last-ditch effort before heading home. Maybe he was supposed to be with Evelyn right now. Maybe that's where he belonged. Strange thing about the Spirit. Things were seldom ever cut and dried.

They drove until the canyon narrowed and its walls grew steep, and then Dill and Brodie walked the edge while Tony drove. They searched for anything unusual—any signs of broken brush or new trails or formations out of place. At a promising spot, the three hiked down into the sage for several yards and spent a good two hours combing every undercut, cave, and thicket along the narrow slope, anywhere a body might be hidden. They found snakes and squirrels and spiders, desert rats and lizards and even a lively tortoise, but, thankfully, no human remains.

After climbing the slope, drinking soda and bottled water in the Suburban, and munching on what was left of the rolls, they continued along the top of the canyon, physically all but finished from their ordeal. At a high point, Brodie stopped the vehicle to look down into the deep brush and into the panoramic vista which lay on the other side one more time. It was a like a finish for him, a feeling of completion. He left Dill and Tony in the car and walked to the overlook by himself. Peering into that endless view of land and sky had always been a little like gazing into heaven. Perhaps that's where Jenny was already, just waiting for the rest of them.

Directly below him, straight down in the brush of the canyon, he caught the glint of something silver in the corner of his eye. Adjusting his stance and looking harder, he saw it again, nearly hidden under the stones and sage, something definitely metal and bright and foreign. Was it an aircraft rudder? Or just an old tin can? Brodie's curiosity was piqued.

The problem was that the piece was a good ways down, mostly covered by underbrush and boulders and impossible to identify from where he stood. Was it worth a rugged hike clear to the bottom of the chasm to find a scrap of metal that was probably someone's discarded bumper?

Brodie looked around, examining the best way down if he should make that choice. Immediately he saw a problem. There was no direct route. No route at all, without looping around or zigzagging several hairpin pathways. They had an adequate rope, he knew, and it crossed his mind to drop Tony down to check, saving the time a hike would take on the rocky, unstable slope. Tony was the smallest of the three and would be easiest to lower on the rope, if he were willing.

Tony was more than willing. He was eager.

"I'm curious as to what that is," Bishop Brodie told him, as they wrapped the secured rope snugly around Tony's waist and belt and as his father pointed him toward his goal. "Just keep your feet against the side and the line good and taut. You'll be okay."

"Got it, Dad. No problem."

He slid down through the brush, falling faster than Rex had intended, and he and Dill had seared rope burns on their palms before Tony got halfway.

After pausing twice to gain a firm position, Tony made it to the level spot at the bottom where the glint of metal shone. "It's big!"

Brodie heard him yell, but he couldn't make out much else from Tony. "What is it?" Brodie called.

Tony didn't respond but spent his time exploring the area while Dill and Brodie waited. When he finally jerked on the line, the sun was dipping low on the swaths of sand, and the bishop knew they'd better hurry. He'd hoped to make it home before the Sabbath ended, for Evelyn's sake. He'd still get there but after dark and with no good news.

Pulling Tony up the hill took more time than any of them counted on, and when he was finally on level ground again, the boy was even dirtier than before. He was thirsty, and his face was scratched and bleeding. What was worse, he was frustrated, having gained little for his efforts. "It was just an old horse trailer," he complained. "It was layin' on its side, all dented and smashed up, like it had rolled off the cliff and bounced ten times or something. A bunch of sagebrush and rock was on it, so you couldn't see it from up here. It was one of those back-wheel jobs that ya hitch to a pickup—a fifth-wheel, I think they call 'em."

Rex Brodie stood stalk still and looked at his son. A striking image crossed his mind. "What color was this trailer?" he asked.

"Silver. At least, at one time. I guess that's why you caught its shine. It was all peeling and warped now. And there was a blue stripe across the side with some words on it. I can't remember what they said. I didn't pay much attention after I saw it wasn't anything to get worked up about." Tony gulped some water from a bottle Dill had handed him. It was getting dark, and he was anxious to go home.

"Find a spot for one more campfire, Dill," said Brodie. "We're sleeping here. I've got to take a look at that trailer come first light."

Bishop Brodie didn't sleep. He paced and prayed in the starry darkness and counted every hour waiting for the sun. There was only one horse trailer he had ever seen that had a blue stripe across it and peeling silver paint.

At the first whisper of dawn, Dillon Dancie and the bishop had started down on foot into the canyon, taking the zigzag route. It was still cold in the desert. The early breezes were crisp and dry, and the smell of sage was sharp on the thin morning air. Brodie's knees groaned as he moved downhill on the rough terrain, but his heart was pumping wildly. He was too excited to be tired, though he hadn't slept. The stark memory that had danced before his eyes all night still pushed him. He only needed daylight and a rambling hike down a rocky hill to confirm what he was thinking.

Suddenly they were there, standing where Tony had been a few hours before. Lying on its side was the horse trailer, hidden beneath the sagebrush and cedar trees. It was scraped and dented, as Tony had described. One corner was completely crushed, and the roof had partially caved in. The silver paint was chipped and peeling, and the stripe across the side had faded from its original navy to a dimmer shade of blue. But stretched across that stripe in silver letters were the words Brodie remembered: *Salt Desert Stampede*. And on close inspection, the bishop found a crooked X distinctly scratched in the blue paint. *Probably done by a corkscrew*, Mike Castle had said.

Brodie looked from the wrecked trailer to Dillon Dancie and back again. He had to take a second to let everything sink in. Dill's eyes widened as he got the drift, and he slammed his fist into his palm. "We saw this outfit a week ago!" Dill cried. "It was parked at Grunwald's place."

"Yeah," said Brodie. "It sure was, and that's where we're headed, as soon as we can make it up this hill!" He was already breathing hard. Some kind of ancient bell was ringing in his ears, an alarm that loving fathers know too well. "Grunwald's!" Brodie kept repeating as he labored up the slope, climbing between the thistles and cedar hedges. "Grunwald's! That's where the connection's always been!" He said breathlessly over his shoulder to Dill as they moved along, "The minute we get in cell range, call Mike Castle and tell him to meet us at Luther Grunwald's place. That fellow has some answering to do."

Chapter Seventeen

WHEN SHERIFF MIKE CASTLE HAD left Brodie and the young men Saturday morning in the west desert, he figured they'd be back home by Sunday evening at the latest. He was aware of the stake fast for Jennifer and the general support across the entire county that weekend. In addition to the Brodies' own ward and stake, other congregations in the vicinity had been touched by the event, for the family was well known and respected. From school and seminary and rodeo club and Young Women activities through the years, Jennifer had countless friends. She came from a large, extended family with cousins from Milford to Tooele, some of whom she hardly knew and only saw at annual reunions. Now many of them gathered, giving Evelyn a collective shoulder to lean on and targeting Sunday as a time to combine their faith and spiritual fervor and plead with heaven to bring Jenny safely home.

Sheriff Castle doubted Rex would miss the special fast meeting, but if he did, Mike intended to take his place and let the assembled people know Jen's father was where he felt he needed to be—still searching, still running down a final lead.

Castle was still busy searching too. Besides drawing up a warrant for the Plymouth, he spent Saturday afternoon combing every record he could find on Bill Muncie. Jennifer's hair in Muncie's truck still didn't make sense to him. Nor did the UHP stop, for that matter. But in his mind, they had to be connected. He did not believe in coincidences, especially one that stretched that far.

The only real piece of progress he made on Saturday was the ten minutes he managed to spend with Muncie's ex-wife, Maxine Davis, who lived in a nice country rambler in Erda. She was a polite, well-groomed lady in her early fifties, and she seemed sincerely sorry over Muncie's suicide.

"I don't know what happened to Bill these last few years," she told Castle, dabbing her eyes with a handkerchief. "He just went crazy over money. He was always looking for another way to make a dollar. And what he made was never enough. It was why I finally had to end the marriage. His greed was more than I could stand."

"Anything illegal that you know of?" asked Castle carefully.

"Not while we were married. But who knows? Something must have been going on for Bill to want to end his life. It really is a shame. He was a fine man for so many years. Even now, I can't see him ever hurting anyone. It's hard for me to believe he'd even hurt himself."

Castle didn't tell Maxine about the hair they'd found in her ex-husband's truck or that it belonged to a young woman who had been missing for six days. Maxine had re-married and done well for herself. He didn't want to make things worse for her than they already seemed to be with regard to her ex-husband. And something about her story had a ring of truth. Bill Muncie was a greedy man but not a killer. Those two pieces didn't fit.

It would take some time to get a warrant on a weekend and have the Plymouth hauled in for a quality search. Castle wasn't sure the investigation would even amount to anything, but he was frustrated by the wait. Whoever talked about the wheels of justice grinding slow must have been a patient man, not an anxious, grieving father, the sheriff mused, thinking of Rex Brodie.

When Brodie still wasn't answering his cell on Sunday, Castle made his visit with Len Gardner to the Grunwald place, then returned home to change into his dress uniform. He drove to the stake center with his wife, Lorraine, in time to accompany Evelyn to the special fast meeting. There were several male relatives with Sister Brodie, but when she saw him, she took the sheriff's arm, obviously wanting to talk.

"Where are Rex and Tony?" she whispered nervously as they took their places at a pew in front. "Don't keep anything from me, Mike. I want to know what you've found." She had a supply of tissues to dab her swollen eyes and wore a pastel summer jacket over a soft white blouse. "Why haven't I heard from Rex?" pressed Evelyn. "Why isn't he here?"

Castle wanted to turn her over to Lorraine and hurry away from her questions, but he knew he had to offer a strong presence. "Rex felt inspired to follow a couple of leads. He should be home soon. To be honest," added Castle, "I would have thought you might have heard from him by now."

Evelyn's eyes widened. Her hands began to tremble. "So there are leads then?" she asked, suddenly hopeful.

"Well, Rex seemed to think . . . that is . . ."

At the pulpit, the stake president rescued him by solemnly calling the meeting to order. "My brothers and sisters," he began, "we have come together today in extraordinary circumstances to partake of the sacrament, to worship together, to plead for the Lord's tender mercies, and to combine our faith and prayers on behalf of a family of this valley whom we dearly love."

During the meeting, Castle looked about at the crowded room. Every seat in the large chapel was occupied, as well as every chair in the cultural hall behind it. People stood in the corners and in the aisles and in the overflow areas between the rooms. They listened as President Lawrence spoke, and they reverently took the sacrament. Castle didn't know where Jennifer Brodie was or if he'd ever find her, but that day he understood the power of community and what sincere empathy could mean when it was multiplied by the love of many.

For the first time in several years, Castle was proud of his religious heritage, proud of this great, unifying faith his fathers had bequeathed to him, those valiant men who had settled in this western desert so long before. He found himself wishing Rex were there to see the great outpouring of support, for he had come to believe that this incident would end badly for the Brodies, and they would need their neighbors, every one.

President Lawrence was an articulate speaker and said many wise and appropriate things to the congregation, but he quoted a verse of scripture from the Book of Mormon that Mike Castle felt was true but ominous.

And now, my sons, remember, remember that it is upon the rock of our Redeemer, who is Christ, the Son of God, that ye must build your foundation; that when the devil shall send forth his mighty winds, yea, his shafts in the whirlwind, yea, when all his hail and his mighty storm shall beat upon you, it shall have no power over you to drag you down to the gulf of misery and endless wo, because of the rock upon which ye are built, which is a sure foundation, a foundation whereon if men build they cannot fall.

The Brodies' sure foundation of faith would get them through this crisis. They could stand against the whirlwind and the mighty storm, Castle knew, and this gulf of misery— losing Jennifer—would not ultimately destroy them. Still, it was a heavy price to pay as proof.

After the meeting, Castle told Evelyn, "I'm going into Salt Lake with Muncie's car early tomorrow. They've got some people there who'll go over it with a fine-tooth comb. Dogs, too, to sniff it out. I still think it's connected."

"His truck didn't give you anything," Evelyn pointed out, "and that's where Bill died."

"I know, but this is different." Castle squeezed her hand, and Lorraine kissed her cheek. "We won't give up," he added earnestly and knew Evelyn believed him.

Chapter Eighteen

AT NINE O' CLOCK MONDAY morning, a truck of dirt and gravel rolled up the road and pulled into the Grunwalds' yard. It was closely followed by a backhoe from the Desert Star Construction Company. The operators of both outfits showed Luther Grunwald some papers and walked leisurely around the mouth of the mine shaft with him for several minutes.

Little Clara Grunwald watched intently from inside the trailer, her bulging blue eyes curious and frightened. She had never seen a backhoe in her yard or anything so large as a truck filled with *that* much dirt. Both vehicles were noisy. Their engines roared with violent power. Clara never took her eyes away, though she pressed her palms to her ears as she watched.

Finally, the truck driver moved his outfit up past the shaft and situated it a few yards from the hole. The backhoe operator followed, aligning his machine in a spot perpendicular to both the dump truck and the pit, where his shovel could swing easily between the two and do its job. There was the usual progression of fits and starts that accompany most projects. The drivers disagreed for several minutes over one thing and then another. Then it seemed there was a problem about how deep to set the truck bed's slant once the fill began to diminish. Then there was another discussion related to the positioning of the bucket.

"Crazy fools!" muttered Luther, coming in the trailer for some water. "Just shovel it in! Fill up the hole with the dirt, and get on outta here!" He grabbed a small ice cooler by the handle and shot a malicious glance at Clara as he turned and darted out the door. "I'll be glad to finally have all this mess off my shoulders," he hissed, "every bit of it buried underneath the dirt of that darned hole!"

Clara toppled anxiously from the chair on which she stood. She hurried into the back bedroom of the trailer and pulled herself up to the curtains to get a closer look. The window, never cleaned, was smeared with mud and dead insects, and even the sun had a hard time lighting up the room. But a dreadful anticipation was filling the little girl. Dropping off the bed and heading for the trailer's door, she dashed outside just in time to see the backhoe's shovel rising up above the dump truck, like some monster opening its jaws and contemplating its first bite of some noble village farmer's good earth. Stupefied, Clara took in the sight. It was almost more than a six-year-old could grasp.

Clara's eyes flew to the shaft, to its mouth there by the rocks. The drivers had helped Luther pull the planks away, and they stood stacked in a pile at the side. The shaft was open now, ready to be filled, plugged up forever by order of the sheriff for the safety of the public. *Shoulda done it a long time ago*, the sheriff had said, *before something tragic happened. These old pits are a symbol of the past, but they are a real danger to us now.* The sheriff's words rang in Clara's ears.

She was mute, not deaf. She never had been deaf. She saw, heard, and remembered.

Frozen in her tracks, Clara tightened her little fists. She looked about for her father and saw him watching the backhoe from several yards away, a satisfied smile on his lips. The shovel's teeth bit into the dirt pile in the truck, a combination of sand and weeds and hard-rock soil, with the gravel to give it heft. The shovel began to shift its lower frame into "gobbling" position, to fill its hollow bucket to the brim. Then, as happens with machines, the engine ground and sputtered to a stop. The truck driver opened the door of the cab and yelled something to the man perched on the backhoe. The backhoe driver hollered back, a foul curse on his lips. He worked the gears and levers of his machine until the engine roared to life again. The jaws shuffled through the dirt, failed to properly close its teeth, and then dropped the load before the engine stopped again, refusing to even purr. This led the truck driver to throw up his hands and exit his cab, seething in frustration. He stomped toward the backhoe and climbed aboard, shouting orders and abuses with every step.

Bishop Brodie's SUV rolled into the yard just as the truck driver managed to get the backhoe started again, and the Suburban momentarily drew Luther's attention. He spit out the stem he was chewing and warily eyed the men that came toward him, not bothering to greet them or tip his hat. The Desert Star Construction Company men paid no interest whatsoever and went about their work as if unaware of any interruption. Clara glared excitedly from the porch.

Dill was the first one out of the car's door, marching up to Luther as soon as he caught sight of the man. "Where's Jennifer, you devil?" he yelled, grabbing Grunwald by the collar when he reached him. "We found your beat-up horse trailer smashed to pieces at the bottom of a canyon twenty miles out. The same one that was sittin' here a week ago. Don't tell us you didn't use it to get rid of Jenny's horse! Where is she, Luther, you lyin' piece-a-trash?"

"Dill!" Bishop Brodie got between them, pulling the young man off Grunwald and helping Luther stand straight again. "Let him be a second. Let him talk."

Grunwald jerked away, fending Dill off with his arm. "Keep that kid away from me!" he growled.

Dill stood back, breathing hard. A few yards behind them, the backhoe's shovel swung into the dump truck for another attempt at the dirt.

"I don't know nuthin' about yer girlfriend," shouted Grunwald. "I told ya that before when ya came around. A fella bought that trailer off the lot after ya seen it. If he drove it off a cliff, that's his problem!"

"What fellow? What's his name?" Dillon's temper was still smoking.

"Danged if I know. It was a week ago."

Dill lurched again at Grunwald, and Brodie had to hold him back.

"What's going on here?" Rex asked, eyeing the backhoe and trying to draw Luther's attention away from Dill.

"I'm doing like the sheriff said and fillin' up that shaft," answered Grunwald, shouting above the noise. "Though they're slow as cold tar doin' it. Must be gettin' paid by the hour or by how dumb they are."

"I'm having a hard time believing you sold that horse trailer so conveniently," said Brodie, looking Grunwald in the eye, "and it just happened to end up where we found it."

"Come clean, Luther!" shouted Dill. "You know more than you're sayin'."

"I don't have to talk to you people." Grunwald shouldered his way past the men and turned his attention back to the dump truck. "You bring a warrant if you want to talk to me."

While the men argued, Clara lingered near. She sidled up behind the SUV, made her way along the back of it, and loitered in Tony Brodie's shadow as he stood watching his father and Luther talk. Mostly, Clara watched with growing fear as the giant backhoe labored over the mound of fill dirt in the dump truck. It gathered up an inadequate load, losing half before its teeth could close, and then began again, to the consternation of the operator and the driver in the cab. Once the shovel actually lifted a full scoop of dirt and was about to swing it toward the shaft, little Clara let out a wail and began throwing pebbles at the backhoe and the truck. None of the rocks went anywhere. The Desert Star men didn't even know they were targets, but Luther Grunwald suddenly went on the rampage.

"Clara! Cut that out, ya little savage!" Striding over to the girl, he sent her in the direction of the trailer with a strong paddle to her backside. "You get in the house and out of the way 'fore you cause more trouble and I skin you good," he roared. "This is men's business." When Clara didn't move fast enough, he scooped her up like squealing pup and marched to the trailer himself. Clara whined and kicked and pointed at the backhoe and tried to wiggle out of Luther's arms. He trudged ahead, opened the trailer door, and pushed her inside, locking the screen against her objections. "Stay in there where you belong!" he raged and turned back toward the yard. "Dang kid," he muttered to the others. "Always gettin' in the way!"

Embarrassed by the man's behavior, Dill and Tony moved away from Grunwald. They began to meander among the cars that sat parked at the far end of the yard, while they watched the backhoe with growing curiosity. The operator was still having trouble manipulating the shovel. Grunwald watched as well, although he kept his distance from Dillon. He knew the kid was seething and was glad of it. He still smirked at the visitors occasionally, leaning against the corner of the barn, a shaded, isolated vantage point. He knew they hated and mistrusted him, but he didn't care. He was glad he could stand apart, knowing what he knew and have the last laugh. His eyes glazed over as he stared at the mouth of the mine shaft. Soon the shovel would swing above it and begin to dump the fill dirt, and the pit would be obliterated, just another heap of rock and sand. And the bonus was it was a secret he could carry to his grave, this thing he knew. The smirk that curled his lips today would always be there for the "better" folks of this valley, the Mormons and the lawmen and the do-gooders and greedy men like Muncie who never wanted to pay a fellow what was owed. It was Muncie's fault at the beginning, Grunwald mused, but the truth was, he didn't like these people. Now his secret would be an ace in his back pocket. He'd have one up on all of them for a good long time.

* * *

Grunwald was right about Dill. Tony could hardly keep him calm. "Let Dad handle this," he pleaded as they stood together, Dill breathing hot and angry. "There's not much we can do till Castle gets here anyway." They were moving among the torn-up cars, kicking fenders, tinkering with exposed plugs, trying to keep their minds off Luther while the sputtering backhoe drew their eyes if not their full attention.

"Castle better get something outta Grunwald when he comes," growled Dill, "or I swear, I'll take the fella on myself!

There's something going on here that has to do with Jenny. I just know it. And I'm not gonna let it go."

The backhoe surged with energy just then, and its revving engine cut off Tony's answer. The shovel dipped low over the truck and grabbed a mighty scoop of dirt and gravel. As the boys watched, it lifted its monstrous head and swung its load toward the hole. This time its aim seemed true.

* * *

Back by the SUV, a troubled Rex Brodie turned his eyes away from the backhoe. He had watched in dismay as Grunwald had wrapped his arm roughly around a frightened and squirming little girl, pushed her into the trailer, and locked the door. Even now, little Clara was pounding with tight fists on the inside of the screen. He could see her face, red, tear-stained, and full of terror, as she wailed for attention.

Brodie didn't believe in coddling children who were having temper tantrums, and he certainly didn't want to step in where he did not belong nor alienate Grunwald. But his heart ached just then in a special way. He loved Jennifer with all his soul. She was *his* little girl. For six days he had searched for her, physically sickened by what his inability to find her probably meant. He had prayed. He had fasted. He had begged the Lord for intervention. He had promised heaven all he had. He would have given anything to see his daughter once again, her sunny smile, her golden hair. To hold her in his arms, he would have sacrificed his life. And here was Grunwald, handling his precious little girl like she was discardable, an animal to be locked away because she was frightened and underfoot.

Moving towards the trailer, he found himself hoping to speak to Clara through the screen, to calm her with a kind word, to let her know that someone cared. He thought he might have to knock to get the little girl's attention, but her anxious eyes met his the moment he got close to the door. She was standing on the other side, her arms extended upward, her hands beating wildly on the flimsy screen.

"It's okay, Clara," he said soothingly, with a quick glance over his shoulder at the backhoe grinding two hundred feet away. "That thing's big and loud, but it won't hurt you." He dropped down on one knee to place himself at her level as he spoke. "That shovel's just filling up the hole out there so no one will fall in. It's a good thing that it's doing."

Clara only wailed and clenched her fists and beat harder on the screen. Her eyes darted back and forth from Brodie to the backhoe. They widened in terror as the shovel, after so much sputtering, finally opened its gigantic jaws and dropped its first load of sand and gravel directly into the shaft, leaving a billow in its wake.

Seeing the dust rise, Clara squealed like a wounded kitten and furiously shook the door. Brodie stared at her, confused. The backhoe's shovel was returning for another load of fill, swinging on its mechanical arm toward the truck. Soon a second pile of sand and gravel would thunder into the shaft.

"Listen, Clara," said Bishop Brodie gently, "I used to have a little girl like you. She's all grown up now, but when she used to be upset or scared, like you are now, I'd tell her stories. That's what I'd do. I'd sit her in my lap and tell her legends and fairy tales and myths. Most of all, I'd tell her all the great stories from the Bible because she liked those the best—David the shepherd boy, Ruth and Naomi, Joseph and his pretty coat—anything she liked to hear. It would always take the fear away, just to have me sit with her like that. If I could, Clara, I'd do that for you now. I'd tell you stories so you wouldn't have to be afraid."

Almost instantly, Clara stopped crying. Her large eyes drilled into Brodie and lit up with the sudden flash of an idea. She turned immediately, scampering into the depths of the trailer behind her, and returned in a moment, her body trembling as she thrust her hands toward the man who waited on the other side of the screen.

Rex could not believe what he was seeing. There in Clara's fingers was the silver dollar from his collection, the Peace Dollar with Lady Liberty on it that he'd given Jenny for her Primary lesson—one of the twenty pieces of silver the merchants used to purchase Joseph from his brothers and to buy his freedom from the pit.

The pit! The pit! The pit! The pit . . . to buy his freedom from the pit!

A shock wave rippled through the bishop's body and left him trembling. "Ohhhhh!" he groaned. "Ohhhh, sweet heaven, no!" With a violent effort he jerked the screen from the wooden door frame and took the dollar from Clara's hands. She looked up at him through tears of childish relief. Fumbling, he turned the coin in his fingers. Then he lurched toward the backhoe, yelling with all the air and strength he had.

"Stop! Stop! There's someone in the shaft! Oh, sweet heaven, stop the backhoe! Stop the bucket!"

* * *

Luther Grunwald straightened where he stood when he saw Brodie running across the yard. His mouth dropped open. For a split second, he was frozen, failing to comprehend just what had happened. He wasn't armed, never considering the backhoe men a threat and knowing Brodie and the others had arrived too late.

"Shut the engine down!" yelled Brodie to the backhoe operator. "Shut it down! There's someone in the pit!"

"What!" the driver bellowed above the roar of the machine. A full shovel was poised over the debris pile in the truck. "What the heck are you sayin'?"

"Shut it down," Brodie repeated, "and don't move that dirt another inch!"

Dill and Tony had raced forward in alarm the moment they saw Brodie head toward the backhoe. Hearing him cry the ghastly words, "Jen's in the hole!" and seeing his twisted face, stirred Dill in just one direction. With fire in his eyes, he found Grunwald and dashed after him across the yard. The man took off like a pistol shot, running around the barn and through the trees that lined the trim grass.

But Dill was full of smoke and rage. He caught Grunwald from behind, there in the cedar trees, tackling him and sending him to the ground in a single lunge. Angrily, he drove his knee into Luther's back and pushed his face into the sand. Never had Dill Dancie felt so powerful or so deaf to another man's plea for mercy.

"Let me up!" sputtered Grunwald. "You're smotherin' me!"

"You low-down devil!" Dillon screamed. "You low-down crazy devil! What did you do to Jenny? What did you do that made you throw her in some hole?"

Grunwald groaned and fought and tried to get away, but Dill single-handedly pinned his arms to cuff him. He used the county-issued bracelets from his own back pocket to make his first arrest as a deputy, though he couldn't have cared less at the time. Soon he had the man shackled by the ankle to a fence post, looking as bitter as a Christmas blizzard. Dill left him there to swelter in the sun. Only one thing mattered now.

The truck driver and backhoe operator had shut things down and left their rigs. They were standing with Brodie at the mouth of the shaft, looking bewildered.

"Get the rope and the safety belt," Brodie told Tony, "and every flashlight we've got." He turned to the workers. "You boys got some kind of a hook or wench on that shovel arm, something that can hold a rope on it good and tight?"

"What's the problem, mister? You say there's someone in the shaft?" The driver was incredulous.

"We're thinking there's a girl down there—my daughter—and we need something to hold a rope. Fast!"

"You're jokin'!"

"Please! We need to drop a rope."

"We can do better than a rope," said the operator, suddenly seeing the urgency of the crisis. "We got a chain we can send right through the center of the bucket, and a power wheel to bring it up and down. It's a darn sight better than a rope."

Soon the operator had the backhoe arm in a locked position directly above the pit, with a thick iron chain secured and running through the bottom of the bucket and hooked to Brodie's climbing belt. Dill was lying on his stomach at the pit's edge, flashing a light into the darkness, calling Jennifer's name but hearing nothing in return. Tony was dropping a light beam of his own as deep as he could make it reach and coupling his voice with Dill's, hoping Jen would hear them.

"You sure she's down there?" said the truck driver incredulously to Brodie, as he helped with the chain. "I hate to say it, but we already dropped a big bucket of dirt and gravel down this shaft, ya know. We had no idea."

"Just keep the chain tight, if you can," said Brodie. He clenched his fists. He was almost too numb to think and had to keep his wits about him.

"Maybe Simmons here should go down," suggested the truck driver. "He's a young guy, built for this kind of thing. He could do it."

The backhoe operator, a hard-muscled fellow in a sleeveless shirt, stepped forward. "I'll go down if you want me to."

"No," said Brodie. "I'll go. I'm Jenny's father. It's me she'll be expecting." There were tears brimming in his eyes as he spoke, bracing himself on the edge of the shaft, the stiff chain ready in his hands. "But thanks," he said. "And someone go get little Clara from the trailer. She shouldn't be alone right now."

With those words, Brodie pushed his feet away and began his descent into the darkness of the pit. *Seven days! Seven days!* His heart pounded wildly over what he was bound to find.

* * *

When the roar of an engine pierced the shaft on Monday morning, Jennifer was too weak and disoriented to be immediately terrified. Only reflex action made her cringe and finally double up against some unknown demon in the darkness. What had happened? Had she died? Where was she? Was this some dark tunnel between heaven and hell, some purgatory of myth and legend, where beasts and monsters bellowed and fires burned and physical pain was excruciating? No, she didn't believe it. She would not believe it! She was surrounded by darkness, certainly. The pain was there. It was almost unbearable. And the roaring sound was loud enough to shake the sand right off the walls. It was frightening, of course, and then mind-numbing. Every time the monster bellowed, a shower of sand poured down on top of her. It covered her hair, filled her ears and eyes and nose, went down her collar. But was this where mortal life had brought her? Is this what she had earned? She would not believe it.

Too many times during family prayer, her father had taken her hand in the circle and thanked God for the beauty of life, for the Atonement of the Savior, and for the blessings that lay in store for those who loved Him. Her faith in those words remained. There was no dark tunnel and no ferocious monster waiting on the other side of the veil. Jennifer continued to drift, sometimes fading, sometimes gaining strength against the turmoil above and around her, which was presently a mystery she could not solve. The sounds? The sand? The debilitating pain? The eye of light above her was wider than she remembered—all the planks had been removed. Was it a part of death or a part of life? She didn't know. But her faith in her father's hand lifting her out of darkness was too much a part of her heart to deny or lose. Often, during her days in the shaft, she would rehearse her first words to her father when he appeared to rescue her. "I knew you'd come," was what she'd say, or maybe, more teasingly, "What took you so long, Dad?"

She remembered falling off a horse once when she was fifteen. The pony was wild and skittish, and Jen was overconfident, bouncing from the saddle when she failed to properly use her knees. The worst of it was that her boot caught in the stirrup, and she ended up getting dragged a good distance before her dad was able to grab the horse and slow him down. The fall was a bad one, knocking her unconscious for several minutes and leaving her back and shoulders with significant road rash. She woke up from that incident not afraid of riding but rather with a renewed appreciation for her father, her emotional faith in him almost ironclad.

During the past week, as she did her best to endure in the darkened pit, that same faith had sustained her. But it was withering with the circumstances. *Hang on! Hang on!* A voice of hope kept whispering in her ear. *Hang on! He's almost here!*

Then a storm descended, a thundering wave of black ash and gravel, rolling over her like an ocean of silt determined to smother everything in its path. Jennifer fought against its overwhelming power, doing all she could in her weakened state to keep her head above the dirt so she could breathe.

* * *

Mike Castle had been five miles out of Salt Lake Monday morning when his cell phone rang. It was Dillon Dancie just getting within range, and he put Rex Brodie on the line right away.

"You remember that silver horse trailer at Grunwald's?" asked Brodie without any sort of greeting. "The one with the blue line through it that said *Salt Desert Stampede* and had an *X* scratched on it? Well, we found that trailer smashed up at the bottom of a canyon out here yesterday. We're headed to Grunwald's now, and he's gonna have the devil to pay. I suggest you join us."

Castle was stunned. But before he could tell Brodie to call Len Gardner and wait until he or the sheriff got there, the bishop had hung up. Castle took the first exit he came to and darted back to the west with his lights on and his siren screaming.

"Grunwald!" he cursed to himself. "'Course it was Luther we should have looked at more. Why didn't we see that silver trailer missing? Stood out like a sore thumb when it was there." Castle hit the steering wheel with his palm and pushed his foot harder to the floor. "Grunwald!" he hissed again. "Hidin' in plain sight!"

Chapter Nineteen

SLOWLY, HIS HEART RACING, REX Brodie lowered himself hand over hand into the darkness of the shaft. He carried glowing flashlights pointed downward on both hips and another on a lanyard around his neck. The beams shot around the walls of the pit as he moved, revealing cold stones and broken ladder pieces and lizard tracks across the sand. He smelled the dust and the stench of many days, and his soul ached as he imagined what had happened here. At the bottom of the pit, while his boots were still braced against the wall and the chain taut, he saw a form reflected in the beam of his flashlight, a girl's body, or part of one—head and shoulders—stuck out from underneath a bunch of dirt and gravel. She was wearing a red-checked shirt that he recognized, though it was smeared with mud and debris. Her long, blonde hair was now black and tangled, her brown eyes only slits, blind in the darkness of the hole.

"Jenny!" Rex swallowed hard.

The girl who lay before him didn't move.

Brodie found a firm place to kneel beside her and quickly adjusted every light he had for its best advantage.

Frantically pushing the dirt away, he took her wrist in his hand to feel for a pulse and pressed his ear to her chest and mouth. Hearing Jennifer moan softly, he lifted her head and whispered her name again. His heart, which had paused in fear, began beating rapidly once more.

"Call an ambulance!" he yelled to the men above, jerking on the chain. "Call an ambulance, right now! And send the rope down. I'll need the extra rope!"

Brodie looked into his daughter's face, now reflected in the light. It was dirty, pale, scratched, and tear-stained but still beautifully alive. "Oh, Jenny," he repeated, "I'm so sorry, baby girl." He put his large hands together on her head, his rough fingers in her tangled hair, and in a voice that was authoritative and commanding, yet no more than a whisper, he began to pray. "Jennifer Evelyn Brodie, in the name of Jesus Christ and by the power of the holy priesthood which I bear, I pronounce a blessing of healing and survival on your soul . . ."

* * *

Mike Castle had just passed the Brodie place south of town when he got the news on his radio. An ambulance had been dispatched to Grunwald's. Then his cell went off.

It was Dill Dancie screaming on the phone, "She's alive, Mike! She's alive!" Dill was breathless and short on details, and he finally gave the phone to Tony, who couldn't do much better. The important thing was clear, and Castle could hardly believe his ears. He slammed on his brakes and made a quick U-turn to head back to the Brodie spread as fast as he could get there, wondering if Tony had already called his mother.

Evelyn was in the yard with several relatives when Castle drove in, his lights still blinking. He could tell immediately she hadn't heard about Jennifer. Her face twisted in terror when she saw him, and her body turned ridged as she grabbed her sister's arm. "You've f—f—found her," she stuttered helplessly to Castle.

"Yes! Rex found her, and she's alive! She's alive, Evelyn! She's alive!" Castle threw his arms around Evelyn and her sister. He laughed and shook hands with every man who stood nearby. He had always viewed himself as a crusty, county sheriff, a cynical guy who'd seen it all. But the day he was able to give Evelyn Brodie *that* good news was the finest of his long career. Her hands flew to her mouth, and her eyes grew wide and unbelieving. Her breathing and her words came rapidly, and Castle's embrace was not only to congratulate but to hold her up.

"I told you she'd come home," cried Evelyn's sister, hanging on to her. "Didn't I tell you that?"

"What's the deal? Where is she?" asked an uncle, and all the others—cousins, aunts, uncles, and friends—gathered around, wanting information.

Evelyn was still shaking. "I've got to call Rex right away."

"I'm taking you to Grunwald's," said Castle. "Your people can follow if they want to, but you're coming right now, with me, and my sirens will be screamin'!"

* * *

And so it was that when Jennifer Brodie was finally lifted out of the shaft that Monday afternoon, those who loved her best were there to welcome her back into the light. Her father, who could have held her tightly in his arms as they were hoisted to the surface, chose to be extra cautious. Using the bottom end of the rope, he made sure Jen was securely tied to his own safety gear, and then, with her head resting on his shoulder, he signaled he was ready, and the wheel above began to turn and slowly pull them to the top.

There might have been clapping and cheering if Jenny hadn't looked so bad. As it was, Dill didn't recognize her. Tony thought that she was dead. And Evelyn, who had just arrived, cried out in shock, running through the men to take hold of her daughter, who seemed no more than a bewildered, dirty, half-dead animal just rescued from a hole. *Seven days! Seven days!*

One of the Desert Star Construction men snapped a picture with his phone just as Jennifer appeared at the mouth of the shaft in her father's arms. Mike Castle studied the photo later, still coming to terms with all that had occurred. At the moment, he stood there numb with disbelief. How many times had he come to this very spot in the last seven days? How many times had he talked to Luther Grunwald? How close had they come to pouring in the fill dirt and burying Jenny in that shaft forever? Great heaven be praised! Thank you! Thank you!

There was much to do, a lot to sort out. Castle had already seen Luther shackled to the fence post, squirming and snapping like a wild rattlesnake. That's who would solve the mystery about Muncie. Grunwald was the culprit here. What he didn't tell them, Jenny would, and that's what mattered now.

Castle took off his hat and ran his fingers through his thinning hair. It was a bright day on the desert. The sun was full and warm, the air as dry as sand. He ignored Grunwald for the moment. There was too much palpable joy at the other end of the yard.

Jennifer lay on a stretcher the paramedics were preparing to lift into the ambulance. IV tubes, oxygen—everything was there. Castle heard something about low blood pressure and dehydration and perhaps some broken bones, but given all that she'd endured, the word "miracle" was not an overstatement. Then Castle saw something in Jen's arm that interested him. Clutched tightly against her chest was an old rag doll, all muddy and torn. Obviously, it had been with her in the hole. *That's odd*, thought Castle, and as he mused about it, his attention wandered to where Tony stood, holding Clara Grunwald up near his shoulder to give her a better view. For the first time Castle could ever remember, the little girl was smiling and that pinch between her eyes had disappeared.

* * *

"None of this was my fault," growled Luther Grunwald across the table from Mike Castle and other authorities in an interrogation room the following day. A public defender was present. "It was that greedy swindler Muncie who tried to cheat me. He started the whole thing." Grunwald's face was sunburned and weary. He looked overwhelmed.

"So you fixed the old Plymouth up to roll a little marijuana in from California, and it didn't quite work out?" repeated Castle for the sixth or seventh time. "I want to hear you say it with your lawyer here."

"You don't have to say anything, Luther," interrupted Charles Beech, the public defender. "You'll get your day in court."

"I don't mind tellin' my side," said Luther. "I shot the greedy cheat Muncie, but he got what he had comin'. That Brodie girl just happened in and saw it. I meant no harm to her. I got scared when she fell in the shaft. That wasn't my intention, and ya shouldn't blame me for it. How was I to know she'd be comin' 'round when she did? She caught me by surprise, and I didn't have time to think. It wasn't anything I planned. Muncie blamed me for leavin' that old license plate on the Plymouth, but it was just as much his fault. Said he wouldn't pay me 'cause he got picked up for those stolen tags. That's a bunch of trash, after all the work I done. I'm sorry for the girl. She mighta been treated poorly. But I still say Muncie got what he had comin', and I ain't goin' back on that."

"I'm advising you to keep quiet about all this, Luther," Beech repeated. "At least for now. We'll get it all straightened out in court. It's better if you let me handle things."

Luther Grunwald threw his hands in the air, just as stubborn and belligerent with his attorney as he was with the sheriff as they took him off to his cell to await arraignment, proclaiming his innocence every chance he got.

Mike Castle watched and listened wearily, taken, as he always was, by the ability of some men to find excuses for their bad behavior. Only, in this case, the behavior wasn't just bad, it was downright wicked. There was no other way to paint it. He was glad that he could tell Maxine Davis better news about her ex-husband. Bill hadn't murdered anyone or committed suicide. He'd been a victim here as well, although not without blemish.

Grunwald was eventually charged with murder, assault, kidnapping, and illegal imprisonment. There was little doubt as to his guilt, and the combined sentences for each charge would keep him incarcerated for the remainder of his life.

It was front-page news the day Grunwald was arraigned, a week following his arrest. The headlines were accompanied by the backhoe driver's cell phone photo of Jennifer coming out of the shaft. Rex Brodie's lined face was a portrait of relief and joy in the picture, and behind him stood a jubilant Dillon and Tony holding a wide-eyed Clara. In the background, Evelyn could be seen running from the car, her mouth open and her arms outstretched, Sheriff Castle just behind.

Mike had been musing over that picture at his desk that morning when he looked out the window and saw old Jake Archer shuffle by. Immediately, he got up and went outside, inviting the man into his office for a chat.

"You seen today's paper, Jake?" Castle asked when Archer was comfortably seated and curiously looking about, having never been in a sheriff's office before.

"No, can't say as I have."

Castle slid the paper across to him. "Take a look at that picture," he said. "That's about the best photograph I ever saw in my whole career of law enforcement. I'm gonna have it framed and tack it up there on my wall."

Archer glanced down at the paper and then bent to look more closely, finally musing over it with great intent. "Yeah, I heard about this," he said. "I heard they found this girl alive . . . in this old mine shaft out at Grunwald's place." He raised his eyes, looking guiltily at Castle.

"I understand you came in here a while back," said Castle evenly, "asking about a reward in this girl's case. Did you have any idea where she was, Jake? Did you know she was out there at Grunwald's in that hole?"

Suddenly, Archer was flustered. He began to fidget in his chair. "No, I didn't know. At least not for sure. I had this dream, ya see. I saw the girl in Grunwald's shaft, plain as day, in the bottom of that pit."

"Well, why didn't you come and tell me about your dream, Jake? Were you holdin' out for money? Were you holdin' out for a reward?"

Archer dropped his eyes, ashamed. "Yeah, I guess I was," he whispered. "I figured that's what I deserved. I figured that gal's daddy would pay a lot to find her, and he'd be offerin' a reward. Luther told me he might, and he made it sound like a good idea."

"Luther told you that?"

"Yeah, so I thought I'd wait for that before tellin' what I knew. I ain't in trouble, am I, Mike? I wasn't sure about it."

"No, you're not in trouble."

"The reward should go to you!" Archer suddenly declared, pointing a gnarled finger at Mike. "You were the fella in charge when the girl was found. You worked day and night to find her. By darn, I know ya did."

"I'm law enforcement, Jake. It's my job. We don't accept rewards."

"Well, ya oughta." Archer was suddenly insistent. "We coulda solved this case together, you and me. I shoulda told ya what I knew right off. Then I coulda got the reward and split it with ya." The man hung his head, ashamed. "That's what I shoulda done. I shouldn'ta let Luther get to me," he said wearily. "You coulda had yer share."

Castle got up, came around the desk, and helped the old man to his feet. "It's okay, Jake," he said gently. "It was only a dream ya had. No clear evidence. But I want to show ya something about rewards." Holding Archer by one arm, Mike directed his eyes to the paper still on the desk. He let his hand float over the photo of the rescue, an image which captured so vividly and unforgettably the elation around the pit. "You see that picture, Jake? Take a good look at it again." While Archer squinted at the photograph, Mike added softly, "That's my reward, right there, the joy on all those faces. That's the only reward that matters, Jake, and it's one I'm glad to share."

Chapter Twenty

IN A HOSPITAL ROOM IN Salt Lake City, Jennifer Brodie sat up against her pillow and looked over the bedcovers at her right leg, set from knee to ankle in a heavy cast. Her shoulder was wrapped too, severely bruised and twisted in the pit, and she'd been treated for other injuries, shock and dehydration among them. Still, Jenny smiled happily. *Thank you, Heavenly Father!* How many times she had whispered those words in the last few days, she couldn't count. She was alive again. She was whole again. She wasn't dirty or thirsty or hungry or in pain. She wasn't alone or cold or in the pitch-black darkness anymore.

Dill came to see her every evening. They sat alone together and discussed their future. He held her hand and smiled at her efforts to tease him over Castle's initial refusal to let him work the case. "Jell-O man? That's what he called you?" asked Jen, grinning.

"I wasn't worth warm custard," Dill admitted, "without you."

"You were tough there at the end, from what I hear."

"Oh, Jen," said Dill finally, "I hope this whole deal's proven the same thing to you as it has to me. I need you. I love you . . . deeply. Sometimes I love you so much I really *do* turn soft when you're not around."

Her lips twisted into a frown. "Dill, I . . ."

"Don't worry, Jen." He laughed. "I'm still going on my mission." He kissed her suddenly with tenderness. "Do you know, I would still go on my mission even if I knew some other guy would have you by the time I got back, and I'll tell you why. I'm going on my mission partly because I'm committed to serve but also because I want to show my gratitude to the Lord for saving you. While you were missing, I promised Him I would. 'Save Jenny, and I'll go,' I said, even if she finds someone new while I'm not here."

Jennifer wept at Dillon's words. They made no verbal commitments. None seemed to be needed.

After Dill was gone, she heard footsteps in the hall, and there at her door stood her mother and her father, smiles on their faces, excitement in their eyes. Between them, holding their hands, was little Clara Grunwald, who raced to Jenny's bedside the moment she came in, letting out a squeal of joy. Clara didn't look quite like herself. Evelyn had bought her a pretty new dress, just her size, with shoes to match. The dress and shoes were multicolored—yellow, red, blue, green—and Jen couldn't help seeing a message there. Evelyn had braided Clara's hair in a fancy style and added a red carnation to the band that held the braid. "You look so cute!" said Jen approvingly, hugging the child. "But you always did to me."

There was the usual fussing over Jennifer's leg, and the necessary back and forth about when she would be coming home. Jen said Dill had been there earlier and would be back again that evening. The bishop told her they were on their way to Brigham City to introduce Clara to some of her mother's relatives. There didn't seem to be too many of them around. But, he added brightly, they'd found one of Clara's mother's cousins who was *very* interested in developing a relationship with Clara and perhaps providing a home for her, if things could be worked out. But Clara needn't worry, in any case. She would always be loved by the Brodies and have a home there to call her own. Luther Grunwald was on his way to prison and was no blood relation to Clara anyway.

Rex lifted the little girl up next to the pillow and let her cuddle in close under Jenny's arm. Jen could tell her father had something ceremonial in mind. He was acting authoritative, like a bishop. First he motioned for Evelyn to join him. Then he looked long and thoughtfully at Jennifer and the six-year-old child lying dreamily beside her. Except for her broken leg, Jen was much herself again, blonde and sunny. She'd turned twenty years old the day before and had the world ahead of her. Rex reached into his coat pocket and took the silver dollar Clara had used to "buy" Jen's freedom from the pit, like the merchants had done with Joseph. Rex had drilled a tiny hole in the top of this silver piece and threaded a ribbon through it. Clara could wear it around her neck if she wanted to. "It's yours," he told her, "and whatever else we can ever give you. Now that we've finally got you to smile, I'm going to see someone about helping you to talk. That's one thing I'm gonna do." He bent and kissed the little girl's forehead and laughed. "I'll bet you've got a lot to say!"

Jen tickled Clara, adding her own grateful burst of joy. "You saved my life, you little angel," she said, "you mysterious, wonderful, little angel." For a moment she toyed with the silver dollar, Lady Liberty, hanging on the ribbon around Clara Grunwald's neck. "A Primary lesson," she murmured. "Who would have ever guessed?"

About the Author

AN AWARD-WINNING PUBLIC SCHOOL TEACHER for nearly thirty years in Southern Idaho, Lynne Larson has written numerous articles, essays, and short stories for both regional and national publications. Since her retirement from the classroom, she has continued to promote education, particularly in history and literature, and is a frequent speaker for book clubs and service groups. She has published six novels, all of which generally reflect her love of Western lore and Americana. A graduate of Brigham Young University, Mrs. Larson also holds an MA in English from Idaho State University. She and her husband, Kent, currently live in American Fork, Utah. They are the parents of three grown children.